Thomas,
hello! I hear
that you are good
in sport and maths.

Brandon
abroad

THE MISSING LEMURS

Hope you like the
story. Maybe we
can meet with your
Dad one morning
and you can tell me
about yourself and

AL MORIN the
book.

All the best,
AL   al.morin2455
@ gmail.co

I AM SELF-
PUBLISHING

@iamselfpub
www.iamselfpublishing.com

Contents

a s we watched the ring-tailed lemurs, something in the distance caught my eye. Two human figures, moving slowly through the bushes. A tall man wearing a black hat and a short man wearing a white hat. The lemur kidnappers! If I didn't act fast, they would get away. So, ignoring common sense, I began following them...

Chapter 1
Nan's Amazing Present

The Golden Toad lived in the forests of Costa Rica. Just five centimetres long, the female was multicoloured and the male was bright orange. The last sighting of one of these colourful amphibians was in 1989. Extinction was caused by a deadly fungus infection and the effects of human pollution.

My family – the Fletchers from London, England – were flying to another holiday destination. Stuck between two sisters – one talkative, the other just plain irritating – I had survived the long flight with the help of a large bag of raspberry bonbons, in-flight cartoons and a good book. I was reading about animals and plants that were extinct or threatened with extinction. I had just finished learning about the Golden Toad. It was a weird thought, the fact that something so beautiful could be gone forever.

"Calling Co-pilot Zecko!"

Eight-year-old Natalie sat in the window seat. During the entire trip, she had been pretending to pilot the plane. Her co-pilot was Zecko the Gecko.

She turned the green hand puppet to face her. "*'Yes, s-s-sir, C-C-C-captain Fl-Fl-Fletcher?'*"

"Anything to report, Mr Zecko?" Natalie commanded in her deep pilot voice. She then pushed the puppet's snout against the aeroplane's small oval window.

"*'W-w-water, s-s-sir. Nothing b-b-but w-w-water.'* "

Fourteen-year-old Hayley, sitting in the aisle seat, looked up from the perfume section of a duty-free magazine. "Natalie, does your stupid puppet *really* need to stammer?"

Mum turned around from where she sat in front of Natalie. "*I* seem to remember a little girl who owned a stuffed panda that constantly sneezed."

"That was different," Hayley explained. "Pandetta had hay fever."

From in front of me, Dad turned to join the conversation. "Why *does* Zecko stammer, Nat?"

"Because when he was a baby, he was chased by a snake. *Nan* told me."

The puppet was a gift to Natalie from our grandmother. Mum's mum. She was always giving us presents. Like this holiday.

*   *   *

I remember that Saturday morning a few months ago. We were all sitting around the kitchen table when Nan announced in her high squeaky voice, "The Fletchers are going to Madagascar!"

"Are you joking, Nan?" I asked.

"I'd never joke about the place where they grow vanilla." Nan was famous for her vanilla sugar cookies, loved by everyone except Hayley. "It's somewhere Derek had always wanted to go." Derek was our grandfather. He died about three years ago.

Mum tried to reason with her. "Mother, you shouldn't be spending all that money on us. *You* might need it."

"For what? A retirement home? Where people sit around all day and watch *Strictly Come Baking Road Show Island*?"

"I think you're mixing up different telly programmes, Nan," pointed out Hayley with an affectionate grin.

"They're all the same! People watching *other* people do things. I mean – they should grab a life!"

"*Get* a life," Hayley corrected.

"Whatever... No, not for me, Alex. It's *my* money and I'll spend it any darn way I please. Like a holiday for my daughter and my three grandchildren."

"What about your sweet, lovable son-in-law?" Dad asked, pretending to be offended.

'Do I *have* one of those?"

Dad scrunched up his face in an idiotic attempt to look sweet and lovable.

"Okay, Julian," Nan said, who really *did* like Dad. "You can come. If you don't ruin it for everybody with all that historical and scientific nonsense!"

"Are *you* coming, Nan?" asked Natalie.

"Maybe on the next trip, Nattie." She patted the top of her left leg. "First, I get a new hip."

"But Mother, what if you want to buy yourself some—"

"Discussion ended," Nan said with finality. She handed Mum an envelope. Inside were five plane tickets and a big wad of spending money.

*   *   *

Autumn half-term break had finally arrived. We flew from London to Istanbul, then changed planes for an overnight flight – across Turkey, the Mediterranean Sea, Egypt, Sudan, Ethiopia and down the east coast of Africa. Seven hours in the air and it was daytime again. For as long as I could remember we had been flying at 30,000 feet over nothing but water.

"Any news, Mr Zecko?" asked deep-voiced Natalie.

Zecko looked out the window. *"W-w-water... w-w-water... w-w-water... l-l-l-land!"*

"Is that Madagascar, Brandon?" Natalie asked.

Outside her window, far below in the vast blue expanse of the Indian Ocean was a smudge of greenish-brown.

"Let *me* see," said Hayley, clumsily leaning over me to have a look.

"Ow!" I yelped.

"Ssshhh, Brandon," Mum said.

"But she – she dug her elbow into my privates," I protested in a hushed voice.

"Well, your privates shouldn't be out in public!" Hayley hissed.

"Very funny," I said. But it wasn't.

"There's not much *forest*," Hayley announced, examining the landscape far below. She shifted back into her own seat to flick through her magazine.

As the plane descended, the smudge of landscape came into focus: farmland, small communities of houses, treeless rolling hills and a jagged peak or two.

"Madagascar is supposed to be *green*," Hayley insisted, stopping at a page in the magazine with expensive watches. "An island full of tropical rain forests."

"It *does* have rain forests," I said smugly, remembering that we had one stop before our final destination. "But that's *not* Madagascar – it's Mauritius, you dodo."

"*What* did you call your sister?" Dad said, turning around to look over his headrest.

"Sorry, Dad."

"Apology not needed, son. I was just wondering because Mauritius was the *home* of the dodo bird. It's probably in your book about extinct and endangered animals."

I quickly skimmed the book's index. *Albatross... Asian elephant... aye-aye... bandicoot... black rhinoceros... coral...* "Here it is, *dodo*, on page 124. "

"It probably won't make for pleasant reading," Mum said.

"Yes," agreed Dad. "In fact, quite gruesome."

I admit I was curious about gruesome things. But my older sister, a future queen of some Satanic cult, was obsessed with them. "Tell us," she begged.

"No, *don't* tell us," said Mum.

"Let's put it to the vote," Hayley said, taking charge of the situation. "Those in favour of hearing about the dodo, put your hand up." Hayley and me. "Those against?" Mum and Natalie.

"Two against two," Dad said. "A draw, so it's probably best that we don't—"

"*W-w-w-wait, Mr Fl-Fl-Fletcher!*" It was Zecko the Gecko!

"Yes? Zecko?" Dad said.

All eyes were on the green hand puppet.

"*I w-w-w-want to hear w-what happened to the d-d-d-d-do-d-d-d-do.*"

"Now just wait one minute," Mum protested. "Natalie, you *didn't* want to hear about the dodo. And Zecko – the hand puppet *controlled* by you – *does* want to hear about the dodo. There's something fishy going on around here. I think that we need a revote. I mean it's only fair if—"

"Sorry, Alex," Dad interrupted. "The results are in... and the official final count – three for hearing about the dodo, two against."

Mum could only say, 'Grrrrrrr!'

Chapter 2

I Can't Believe We're Here!

Dodos were native to Mauritius, an island in the Indian Ocean. Lacking predators, these large flightless birds had been living in safety for over four thousand years. Unfortunately for them, European sailors reached Mauritian shores in the early 1600s. Unaware of the danger, the harmless dodos were easily hunted – killed for food and sport. Seventy years after the arrival of humans, the dodos were gone.

"I want to ch-ch-change my v-v-v-ote."

I agreed with Zecko. It was upsetting to hear about the dodos. I wasn't a vegetarian like Natalie so I was alright with the fact that the sailors needed to eat. But to kill the friendly birds for *sport*?

"Are extinctions always our fault?" Natalie asked.

"No, Natalie," Dad said. "Long before we were around, animals were wiped out by *natural* forces. Ice ages, rises in ocean temperature. The asteroid that killed off the dinosaurs. Unfortunately, the arrival of humans has spelt disaster for many more living things."

Like the poor dodo birds.

After landing in Mauritius, we stayed in our seats, watching some of the passengers get off the plane.

A young couple speaking with a Scottish accent walked past and Mum winked at us.

"Mauritius is a popular honeymoon destination," she whispered.

"Honeymoon? That's disgusting!" said Natalie.

"You don't even know what that means," challenged Hayley.

"I do so!"

"Oh, yeah? What is it, then?"

"A honeymoon is when a man and lady get married and go to another country and sit on a beach and drink champagne and stare at each other and hug and kiss... for a whole week!" Natalie then coyly tilted her head and gazed at me with wide-open, puppy dog eyes. "Oh, Brandon. I love you, I love you, I love you!"

"Well, I don't love *you*!" But I couldn't help but laugh along with the others. Both Natalie and Hayley could be quite funny at times.

As fresh passengers boarded the plane, I looked out the window, squinting in the late afternoon sunshine. There was a silver fuel tanker, driving along the runway tarmac towards another plane. A flatbed trolley with massive white bags moved in the opposite direction towards the terminal building.

"I wonder what's in those *boxes*?" Natalie asked, pointing out the window. Stacked on the tarmac were some large wooden crates.

"Brandon. How many are there?" Dad, now looking out my window, was always giving me mathematical challenges.

I couldn't see all of the crates as they were stacked as a cuboid. But I knew the formula. Let's see... four long, two wide and three high – with two extra ones on top: 4 x 2 x 3 + 2... "Twenty-six!"

"Well done," Dad said. "I guess for you that was an easy one."

Natalie repeated her question. "Twenty-six boxes of what?"

"Soap!"

The answer came from a tall man walking down the aisle. He was dressed in a navy-blue uniform. Attached to his peaked cap was a metal pin in the shape of a pair of wings. On his jacket, he had a name badge that read CAPTAIN YILDIZ. (I guessed that he was Turkish: he looked Turkish and flew a Turkish Airlines plane.)

"Yes, twenty-six boxes of soap." The pilot stopped beside our seats.

"Soap?" I repeated.

"Yes," said the pilot. "It's something people use to wash themselves."

Natalie burst into giggles.

The pilot smiled at me. "My friend, I am just joking with you. Yes, those crates always—"

"Speaking of jokes –"Hayley said, "*A man walks up to the airlines' desk and asks to buy a return ticket. 'Where to?' asks the ticket agent. 'To right back here!' the man says.*"

"That is a good joke," said Captain Yıldız.

"Thanks," said Hayley. I have another one. '*Sitting next to each other on a plane is an English zombie, a French Zombie and a German zombie. This big fat guy comes walking down the aisle and—*"

"Captain Yıldız," Mum interrupted, "you were telling us about those crates."

"Yes. Every Saturday twenty-six crates filled with soap fly from Mauritius to Madagascar. And every Wednesday the same twenty-six crates leave Madagascar for Mauritius, empty of soap but now filled with T-shirts. From there they go to many countries to be sold as souvenirs." The captain looked at his watch. "Sorry, I must return to work. If I don't fly this plane to Madagascar, I will have to deal with a family of five very angry English people!"

Captain Yıldız said goodbye and walked down the aisle towards the front of the aeroplane.

"I can't believe we're here!"

We all agreed with Mum. After a 90-minute flight from Mauritius, we touched down in Madagascar. The place on the travel posters. The place in TV nature programmes.

The sun was low in the sky when we stepped out of the airport terminal building. A young man was waiting for us with a sign that said, "The Fletchers". Our guide. Though not very tall, he was quite muscular, with light brown-skin and closely cropped hair. Speaking English softened with a French accent, he introduced himself as Hery Rakoto. "Welcome to the capital of Madagascar – Antananarivo." He looked to Natalie. "Can *you* say that?"

"Ana – anatna – antarava – anarivo..." she said, her floundering attempts drowning in her giggles. "I can't pronounce it!"

"*We* have trouble too!" Hery confided. "So, we say 'Tana'. Welcome to Tana!" Hery picked up five or six pieces of our luggage and we followed him across the airport car park.

After our luggage was packed into a blue minivan, we climbed inside. Mum sat in the front next to Hery. Behind them were Dad and Hayley. Then came me, Natalie and Zecko. Hery started the van and we drove off.

The long trip from London had been exhausting. That's why the drive from the airport to the city centre lacked the usual Fletcher comments. Dad didn't give us a long lecture on Madagascar's history. Mum didn't comment on the motorcycles and yellow taxis going too fast. Hayley didn't make any sarcastic comments about all the rubbish on the ground. And Natalie didn't ask any old question that happened to pop into her head.

I gazed out the window at the colourful billboard ads. Some were familiar – Gillette razor blades, Duracell batteries, Ariel laundry detergent, Laughing Cow cheese – while there were others I had never seen before, like the many adverts for THB, a beer with three horses on a red label.

The traffic increased as we approached the outskirts of the city. There were more people walking about. As I tried to keep my eyes open, questions wandered aimlessly through my mind. *Would we see any lemurs? Will I like the food? Did I pack enough underwear?*

And, like the last three holidays – *was I in for a new mystery?*

Chapter 3

The Strange Old Man

For 165 million years, dinosaurs dominated the Earth. Then 66 million years ago, an asteroid struck the planet. The tremendous explosion produced changes in the atmosphere and oceans that were lethal to three-quarters of all living things, including most of the dinosaurs. Those few surviving dinosaurs had feathers. Over the next millions and millions of years, these creatures would evolve into birds.

My rambling thoughts were interrupted by a strange noise. Like the trumpeting of an elephant, but higher-pitched and longer-lasting.

"What the hell was that?!"

"Hayley!"

"Sorry, Mum... What the *heck* was that?!"

Again, we heard the trumpeting noise.

"Please excuse me," Hery said. Without taking his eyes off the road, he removed a mobile phone from his shirt pocket. The sound had been his phone's ringtone. He answered the incoming call, made a few monosyllabic responses, then returned the phone to his pocket. "My mother," Hery explained, smiling with embarrassment. "Reminding me to put petrol in the minivan."

"Your ringtone," I said. "What *was* it?"

"The call of the indri. One of Madagascar's many lemurs. It is my favourite."

A few weeks ago we saw a television programme about lemurs. The fossil record shows that these mammals were around 60 million years ago. And then evolution took over. Evolution explains how living things change bit by bit over millions and millions of years. Some lemurs became monkeys. Some monkeys became apes. Some apes became the Fletchers.

Yes, lemurs are our prehistoric ancestors. Tomorrow we were going to see some of these lovable, furry relatives. But first, we needed to find our hotel. The sun had set, leaving the city bathed in soft twilight. Tana, smaller than London, was encircled by hills. The traffic now moved slowly, drivers mindful of the many pedestrians crossing the streets.

"Look at all the Madagascar people!" said Natalie.

"We say *Malagasy* people, Miss Natalie. That is the word to describe most things on the island of Madagascar. And you are right. The people are coming from the busy outdoor market. It is closing for the night."

Most of the people were carrying full plastic bags. The women wore flip flops and knee-length skirts and were wrapped in shawls. Men were in trainers, jeans and T-shirts, their heads covered with straw hats or baseball caps.

Eventually, we left the market area. It was growing dark. As we wound our way up into the hills, Hery gave us a quick lesson in Madagascar's history.

He explained how boat people from the east came to the island two thousand years ago. Later, farmers from Africa sailed here from the west. And later still, from the north, the ships with Arab traders arrived. By the 1500s the Europeans had discovered the island: Portuguese, Dutch, English and finally the French, who forcefully took over in 1883. France ruled the island until 1960.

"Is that why you speak French?"

"Yes, Miss Natalie," Hery answered, turning onto a narrow potholed side road. "French is still taught in many secondary schools."

"Our *hotel* is definitely French," Dad added. Halfway down the poorly-lit street, we could just make out a sign showing three olden-day swordsmen wearing wide-brimmed hats with feathers: *Les Trois Mousquetaires.* Soon we were unloading our luggage outside *The Three Musketeers* hotel.

Although night had fallen, we had attracted a small group of souvenir sellers. A girl (younger than Natalie) with chameleon keychains. A teenage boy selling T-shirts with a map of Madagascar on them. A young woman with a baby strapped to her back, pleading with us to buy a white tablecloth embroidered with flowers.

Hery said something in Malagasy – the island's native language – and the sellers dispersed. "There are many poor people in my country," he told us.

I then noticed that one seller had not walked away. Standing near the minivan was an old man, tall and thin. His face was weather-beaten and dark, a sharp contrast to his well-groomed, vanilla-white beard. He wore sandals, brown trousers and a brown collared shirt. On his head was a brown straw hat.

Most unusual were his eyes. Even in the dark, you could see that they were *red*. And they were staring right at *me*.

Hery again spoke to the man, his tone respectful but insistent. Hery repeated a phrase... and the old man resignedly began drifting away.

Then he paused, turned around and walked back towards us. He stopped directly in front of me. In his outstretched hand was an object that I hadn't seen before. A transparent packet. Photographs. Animal postcards.

When on holiday, I often bought postcards for my drawing hobby. On the wall in my bedroom in London, there were several drawings from past adventures: a boat-filled harbour in Turkey, India's Taj Mahal, extinct woolly mammoths from the south of France.

The old man extended the pack of postcards towards me. I stupidly patted my shorts in a feeble attempt to show I had no money (which was true, as Dad hadn't given us any spending money yet).

The man smiled – it seemed like a sad smile – then pushed the pack of postcards into my hand. "Please..." he said without a detectable accent, in a tone I couldn't figure out. Then the old man with the red eyes, white beard and brown straw hat turned and disappeared into the night.

We all stood there for a few seconds, trying to make sense of what had just happened.

Dad broke the silence with a loud yawn. "Well, Brandon, looks like you have yourself a free souvenir. C'mon, everybody," he said, picking up his suitcase. "Time for a quick bite to eat and an early night."

I slid the pack of postcards into my shorts pocket. As I followed Dad and the others to the hotel entrance I thought about the old man's single word: "Please..." Was it a simple gesture of an offer, as in *Please take this*?" Or was the "Please..." a request for help? And if so, *why* did he need help? And why from *me*?

Chapter 4
It's all about the animals

Woolly mammoths, known for their thick fur and long curved tusks, once roamed the cold lands of Europe, Asia and North America. Survivors on Earth for hundreds of thousands of years, many died in the freezing conditions of the last ice age. The few remaining animals were probably hunted to extinction by early humans.

The next morning, I was woken up by Dad. "Everybody have a good night's sleep?" he said, standing in the hotel room where my sisters and I were staying.

"What time is it?" I yawned, slowly sitting up and stretching my arms.

"Not a simple question," Dad said, shifting to his professorial tone of voice. "According to Albert Einstein, time is *relative*. This is nicely illustrated in the case of twins, where one sibling remains on Earth and the other travels *away* from the Earth at the speed of light. According to Einstein *his* clock will—"

"Dad, it's too early for stupid old Einstein!" That was Hayley's mumbled voice from under the sheet in the bed near the window.

"Speaking of *old*," I said, "did I dream that some old man gave me a pack of postcards?"

"It wasn't a dream, Bran." Dad picked up something from the floor near my crumpled clothes. "Here's a ring-tailed lemur to prove it." He handed me the postcard. "It really happened."

"Why were his eyes red?" Natalie asked, popping up like a jack-in-the-box from her bed nearest the door.

"I'm not sure, Nat. Possibly from lack of sleep. Or he could have an infection..."

"I bet... he was an alien," Hayley said.

"And how do you know aliens have red eyes?" Dad challenged. "Have you seen one?"

"She *has* seen an alien, Dad," I said. "Every time she looks in the mirror!"

Natalie thought this was hilarious.

"What's so funny?" Mum was now standing in the room.

"You don't want to know," Hayley said.

"You're right, I don't," Mum agreed. "I want breakfast, and then I want to begin exploring this wonderful country."

Having slept late this morning we were the only ones eating in the hotel restaurant. The red-carpeted room had about a dozen tables plus a bar with a bracket-mounted television. On the walls were large, framed photos of Madagascar. Outside the large window, we could see a small swimming pool.

Breakfast now nearly over, Dad had just given us our pocket money and was discussing the trip. Only half-listening, I flicked through my postcards – eight different lemurs – while working on my fourth piece of toast.

"So. Any questions about the itinerary?" Dad asked. "Yes, Hayley?"

"Is this another holiday where we get dragged to boring old museums?"

"I like museums," countered Natalie. "Remember those Neanderthals, Brandon?"

"Huh? Neanderthals? Oh, yeah." In France, there was a museum diorama with life-sized prehistoric people.

"They were *spooky*," Natalie said.

I picked up toast number five, smiling to myself. (Only *I* knew *how* spooky they really were.)

"'No' is the answer to your question, Hayley," Dad said. "We're mostly outdoors on this trip."

"Will we see any fossas?" Natalie asked. "I want to see a fossa."

Fossas were mongoose-like animals. In the animated film *Madagascar*, they were the lemurs' enemies.

"I hope so," Dad said. "Yet I hear they're quite shy. Tend to keep well hidden."

"How about orchids?" Mum asked. "Is this the right season?" Mum loved flowers, especially orchids. (She told us about one single flower that cost £4,000!) Madagascar was known for its beautiful orchids.

"Sorry, Alex," Dad said. "No orchids this time of year. How about you, Brandon?"

"How about me *what*?"

"Have any questions?"

"Er – yeah... yeah, I have a question." I hesitated, then pointed to the almost empty plate in the middle of the table. "Does anybody want that last piece of toast?"

"I still don't see many trees," Hayley said, gazing out the minivan's window. In the past half hour, Tana's houses, shops, churches and outdoor markets had given way to open farmland and the occasional dusty town. We were on our way to a nature reserve, a sort of a safari park for lemurs.

"You are right, Miss Hayley. Before people arrived, the whole island was covered in trees." Hery pointed towards distant rounded hills, pale brown and bare, except for tiny patches of dark green. "Now, ninety per cent of the forest is gone. It is a big problem."

"*Why* is it a big problem?"

I knew the answer to Natalie's question. "Less trees mean that—"

"*Fewer* trees," Mum corrected me.

"Huh?"

"If you can count them one by one, it's 'fewer', if you can't it's 'less'. *Fewer* trees, *less* forest."

"You sound like my older brother, Mrs Fletcher," Hery said, with a big smile on his face. "He writes

We nodded enthusiastically.

Keeping his eyes steady on the road, Hery began his tale.

Chapter 5

Postcard Number Six

Neanderthals lived in Europe, the Middle East and Asia. Intelligent and creative, these humans made tools, planned organised hunting expeditions and cared for their fellow Neanderthals. Evidence from fossilised skeletons indicates that they spoke a simple language. Having survived for 400,000 years, the last Neanderthals died out 40,000 years ago. Their extinction was probably due to climate change, disease and deadly warfare with other humans – the ancestors of humans living on Earth today.

"A long time ago – long before there were lemurs or humans in the world – there was a group of creatures living deep in Madagascar's forests. They lived in the trees but could also move across the ground, walking upright on their two hind legs. They worked hard to survive, spending much of their time looking for food and hiding from predators. But for many many years, they were happy.

The creatures were ruled by two wise brothers, who we will call Brother A and Brother B. One day Brother A found his sibling sitting on a log, sobbing loudly.

'What is wrong, Brother B?'

'I am so tired, Brother A. All day long we look for food. We hide in fear from birds of prey and snakes. At night we shiver in the cold.'

'What else can we do?'

'I have an idea. To start a new life.'

'A new life? What do you mean?'

'We can leave the forest. You, me, our families. We can build warm houses. Grow rice. Keep animals for milk and cheese and meat.'

'A house needs wood,' said Brother A. 'That means cutting down trees. For growing rice and raising animals, the land must be cleared. That means cutting down more trees. The trees are our homes.

Our friends. No, it is not a good idea to leave the forest."

But Brother B's mind could not be changed. He had made his decision. 'I am sorry, Brother A... but I must go away.'

'I am sorry, too.'

So, with tears in their eyes, the brothers hugged each other for the last time. Brother B and his family left the forest and travelled far away. They cut down trees, clearing the land for rice and farm animals, using the wood to build houses and keep warm.

Brother A remained in the forest. He and his family spent all day looking for food. They hid in fear from the birds of prey and snakes. At night they shivered in the cold.

Many years went by. The descendants of Brother B had turned into people, the descendants of Brother A had turned into lemurs.

The humans completely forgot their past, their connection with their family deep in the forest. They continued cutting down trees, making it more and more difficult for the lemurs to survive.

One of the lemurs – the indri – never forgot the ancient family bonds. To this day the indri cries every morning, a cry filled with the pain of that day when he and his brother parted ways forever."

Hery's story ended.

"That was so sad," Natalie said.

It was sad. We continued our drive to the nature reserve in thoughtful silence.

I wasn't very comfortable with that kind of emotional silence, so I got things going again. "Hery, how many different kinds of lemurs *are* there?"

"Many," said Hery. "One hundred and five species."

"Do you know the *names* of any of them? I asked.

Hery just smiled.

"*All* of them?" Hayley asked.

"Even *Archaeoindris fontoynontii.*"

"Archa*what*?" asked Natalie.

"I am just showing off, Miss Natalie. "That lemur is extinct. I suppose I *do* know my lemurs. Some children are dinosaur crazy, some are football crazy. When I was a boy, I was *lemur crazy.*"

"Test him, Brandon," Dad urged.

The postcards were in my lap. I picked up the top one, describing what I saw in the photo. "*I am black and white... I have long legs. My eyes are green. Who am I?*"

"Easy," said Hery. "Our good friend, the indri."

I placed the postcard at the bottom of the pile. The second postcard showed a lemur at night clinging to a slender tree trunk. *"I am nocturnal. I am small and brown. My face looks like a bat with really big ears and red eyes. I have long fingers..."*

"You are the aye-aye."

"I know *them*," Hayley said. "The ones with the long skinny middle finger. They're so cute!"

"And wise," Hery said. "My grandfather believed that aye-ayes live high in the trees so they can keep watch over all the other lemurs."

I quickly moved on to another postcard. *"I like walking on all fours. I have a grey body with black circles around my eyes. My long, black and white striped tail sticks straight up into the air!"*

"Ah, yes, the famous ring-tailed lemur.."

"Julien!" shouted Natalie. Dad's name – Julian – was pronounced the same as the film's king of the lemurs. Having not seen the film, Dad looked at Natalie in confusion. "From the *Madagascar* movies, Dad."

"A very good film," said Hery.

Natalie, Hayley and I – and Hery – broke into wild singing:

"I like to move it, move it...
I like to move it, move it...
I like to move it, move it.
Ya like to – move it!"

After a couple more (identical) verses, we ended our fun and I picked up another postcard. *"I am tiny, but I have a long tail. My fur is brownish-grey with some white on my tummy. I have large brown eyes and small pointed ears..."*

"Ah, yes. I have held you in the palm of my hand! You are Mrs Berthe's mouse lemur!"

I skimmed the notes on the back of the postcard: *smallest primate in the world... 9 centimetres long... weighing just 30 grams*!

Hery was halfway there to a perfect score. I picked up another postcard. *"I am brownish grey with small round ears. I look very friendly and my tail is very long...."*

"That is a difficult one," said Hery. "There are many brownish-grey lemurs with small round ears... but I will say... I will say that you are a bamboo lemur."

"Right, but which one?"

"You are a tough quizmaster, Mr Brandon! I will say... that you must be... the... the eastern lesser bamboo lemur."

I nodded my head, indicating that Hery was right again.

"Wow, Hery, you know every lemur in the whole world!" Hayley exclaimed.

"Thank you, Miss Hayley."

Hery signalled right. He turned off the main road onto a dirt track.

"Time for postcard number six." I examined the next card, a photo of two lemurs huddled together on a branch. "*I have green eyes. I have small, rounded ears. My fur is brown except for a white, star-shaped patch on my forehead...*"

Hery didn't answer immediately. Then speaking slowly, he said. "I... I don't know."

Impossible, I thought. "Are you sure, Hery?" I asked. "It's got that white star on its forehead."

"Yes, I am positive, Mr Brandon. This lemur is unfamiliar to me. What is its name?"

I turned the postcard over. In the space where the other cards had information, there was nothing. It was completely blank.

"I... I don't know either, Hery. It doesn't say."

"Let's see," Hayley said, snatching the card out of my hand. "Brandon's right," she said, holding up the blank postcard for everyone to see.

"That's odd," Mum said.

"I guess someone made a printing mistake," Dad suggested.

Dad was probably right. I have a friend named Noah Ludwig who has a Pokémon card with the picture printed upside down. (He also, like me, has two crazy sisters – Emmy and Lucy). Apparently, the card is worth a lot of money.

I described the lemurs on the final two postcards — and Hery knew them immediately: a red ruffed lemur and a golden-crowned sifika.

"Seven out of eight, Hery," Mum said. "Very impressive."

"Yes... but I am still troubled by the lemur I did not know."

"You're getting old, Hery." Hayley teased. "Like Dad, your memory's starting to fail."

"There's nothing wrong with my memory," Dad objected. Then, looking around at us in mock confusion and fear, he added, "Who *are* all of you people?!"

The others laughed. I only managed a smile as I was too busy thinking about the mysterious postcard.

Chapter 6

What's Inside that Little House?

archaeoindris (arkee-OH-in-dris) was the largest lemur that ever lived. Despite being the size of a male gorilla and having the face of a grizzly bear, it was a shy creature. A vegetarian, it spent most of the day eating leaves in the high canopy of Madagascar's forests. Archaeoindris became extinct around 2,000 years ago. Its slow-moving, unsuspicious nature made it easy prey for human hunters.

The track ended at a high metal fence where there were several parked vehicles. Hery slotted the minivan between a small red car and a white tourist coach. We got out and stretched.

Near the fence's closed gate was a wooden sign: LEMUR CONSERVATION CENTRE.

"Is this where they teach lemurs how to *talk*?" Natalie asked as she did a few sloppy star jumps.

"Not *conversation*, Nat," Dad said as he looped the strap of his new, expensive camera around his neck. "*Conservation*."

"That means caring for the environment, Nat," Mum said.

Hery agreed. "In Madagascar, we have many rare and precious animals."

"Like *me*!" The new voice belonged to the young black woman now walking towards us. She was short and slender, with long hair and large brown eyes.

"You're ten minutes early, Mr Rakoto," she said to Hery.

"Ten minutes – but how did—"

"Your mother called." The young woman turned to us. "Hello, my name is Tatiana." She then turned back to Hery. "She said you would arrive exactly at twelve." Tatiana explained that Hery's mother always lets her know about her son's whereabouts. "She would like Hery and me to go on a date."

46

"Date?" Hery said, laughing. "My mother usually goes straight to, 'When is the *wedding*?'"

"And there's no way I'm marrying *him*." Tatiana looked at Natalie. "In Grade 1 he called me Pygmy Hippo... just because I was a bit short."

"*Very* short. *And* fat," teased Hery. "Anyway, she called *me* Coconut Brain!"

Now Tatiana addressed Hayley. "What would *you* call someone who always forgot 'seven' when he counted to ten?"

"I'd say... a coconut brain," Hayley said. "Definitely a coconut brain."

She thanked Hayley for her opinion and smiled triumphantly at Hery.

Tatiana unlocked the gate and we followed her through to a small education centre, a one-story building badly in need of a fresh coat of paint. Once inside, we sat on fold-up metal chairs in front of a wall-mounted TV screen. Tatiana touched the keyboard of a nearby laptop computer and the dark screen came to life. It was a film entitled, *A SPECIAL ISLAND*.

"*Our home...*," voiced the film's unseen narrator. "*...a long, long time ago.*"

"Huh?" exclaimed Natalie, surprised by the animation.

On the Earth on the screen, all the land was in the middle of a giant ocean. It was squashed together into one massive blob. At the bottom, it said 300 MILLION YEARS AGO. Time moved forward: 275, 250, 225... and as time passed, the landmass ever-so-slowly moved. It began breaking up into large pieces. A young child's jigsaw puzzle coming apart. At 180 MILLION YEARS AGO Africa was recognisable. A piece from Africa broke off fifty million years later: the island of Madagascar.

There was still some movement as other pieces of land drifted in various directions. When the yearly countdown had reached 0 – TODAY, the map looked like the one hanging on the wall in my class at school.

The next part of the video was a cartoon showing animals arriving from Africa fifty million years ago. Lemurs, chameleons and other creatures floated across the ocean on rafts made from branches and other vegetation. The film jumped to more recent history – the migration of people that Hery had explained.

The last sequence on the film showed a colour-coded map of Madagascar. Green marked the forests. 2,500 years ago, the island was *covered* in forest. Then the people came. The green slowly disappeared. Today's map was mostly white with small bits of green, the last refuges for the forest animals.

When the film ended Dad whistled with amazement. "That last map says it all. No wonder the lemurs are endangered."

"How much danger are they *in*?" asked Natalie.

Hery explained that the word 'endangered' is when the number of animals gets smaller and smaller. If the situation gets worse, the animals become 'critically endangered' – which is close to being 'extinct'.

"Yes," said Tatiana grimly. "No trees, no leaves and fruit to eat. No place to hide from predators."

"Predators?" I asked.

"Birds of prey. Human hunters. And of course, the—"

"Fossas!" Natalie shouted out.

"Yes," said Tatiana. "But in the Malagasy language, it's not pronounced 'foss-a', it's pronounced '*foo-sa*'."

"Is the film true?" asked Natalie. "Do they kill lemurs?"

"Yes, they do," said Tatiana. "But not many. We, humans, are the real problem."

"*Some* humans must be trying to help?" said Hayley.

Hery pointed a finger at Tatiana.

She smiled modestly. "Many people *do* care. There are wildlife reserves like this all over the island. Some for mammals. Some for reptiles or birds. Here we protect five different species of lemur." She pointed at the door. "Shall we see if they're around?"

We left the education centre and crossed a bridge that spanned a stream of slow-moving water. "This man-made watercourse borders the park and stops our little friends from escaping," explained Tatiana. "Lemurs hate the water."

"Except for the lesser eastern bamboo lemur," corrected Hery. "They enjoy swimming."

Tatiana jerked a thumb in Hery's direction. "Can't count to ten – but he knows his lemurs!"

Tatiana led us through the trees to another small building. This one was newer than the education centre. The walls had a clean coat of green paint and the slanted roof was covered with new-looking red tiles.

"Please come in here," she said, unlocking the door for us to enter. "I will show you something very special."

This sounded interesting.

In one corner of the room, there was a metal desk covered in papers, a microscope, a laptop computer and a dirty coffee mug. Filling most of the rest of the room was a large cage made from chicken wire. Inside the cage was a vertical wooden structure slightly resembling a tree with branches. There was also a small house, like the wooden huts for animals in the zoo. A ramp sloped up from the floor to the dark square opening in the front of the hut.

"What's inside that little house?" Natalie asked.

From inside the hut came a rustling sound. Then, at the opening, a pair of green eyes. Tatiana made a low, soft clucking sound. A face – the face of a lemur with small, rounded ears – peered out of the opening. And a second face. "They were found two nights ago. In a small forest up north. Both were sick."

"What kind of lemurs are they?" I asked.

"We don't know."

"What?" said Hery, "You mean – you mean, they're a—"

"Yes. A new species."

Two cat-sized blurs of brown exploded from the hut's opening – along the ramp and up to the top of the tree-like structure.

"They're so cute," said Natalie.

The lemurs stared down at us – wary, yet with curiosity.

"You are their first tourists," Tatiana said.

And then I had a good look at these newly discovered primates. Green eyes. Brown fur. A white, star-shaped patch on their foreheads.

The lemurs on that postcard!

Chapter 7

A Close Call

Long ago, a group of pygmy hippos swam across the shallow ocean channel that once lay between Africa and Madagascar. The Malagasy pygmy hippos made Madagascar their home, surviving peacefully for hundreds of thousands of years. Unfortunately, humans came to the island and the pygmy hippos were hunted to extinction.

No wonder Hery wasn't able to name number 6 in my lemur quiz. Nobody knew that it even *existed!* There were no looks of surprise on the faces of Mum, Dad or my sisters; I guess they hadn't made the same connection between the living creatures perched above us and the ones on my postcard. *Hery* had noticed. His eyes met mine, eyebrows raised with questions neither of us could answer.

"It's so cool being the first ones to see them," Hayley said.

"Do they have names?" Dad asked.

"No *scientific* names yet," Tatiana said. "I call them Romeo and Juliet. And they love eating this." From her pocket, Tatiana removed a small plastic bag with pieces of mango. First, one lemur, then the other, scampered down the wooden structure and reached out with a delicate human-like paw, plucking the fruit from Tatiana's fingers before shooting back to the top where they could eat it in privacy.

Tatiana asked Hery something in Malagasy.

"Tatiana would like to take a photo of the lemurs and their first visitors. For the reserve's website."

Standing in front of the cage, we smiled as Tatiana used her phone to take a photo. Apparently losing interest with their human company, the lemurs climbed down from the top of the branch-like structure and disappeared into their wooden hut.

"What will *happen* to them?" Hayley asked as we continued our walk through the wildlife reserve.

"Hopefully, one day they will be released. Back into the forest."

"But many cannot live in the wild," Hery said.

"Yes," explained Tatiana, "Most of the lemurs here were kept as pets."

"Pets?" I asked.

"Yes, rich people in Madagascar – and all over the world – will pay good money for exotic animals," Tatiana explained.

"To show off to their rich friends," added Hayley.

"Exactly," said Tatiana. "It's bad enough that people keep the animals locked up. It gets worse when the owners become bored with their new pets. They drive them somewhere and dump them. Most of them were bred to be pets and have forgotten their survival skills. The lucky ones are found by kind people who bring them to us."

"You mean the lemurs here in the forest are *tame*?" Natalie asked.

A rustle of leaves from above was immediately followed by the sight of a falling brown blur – which landed with a hard plop on Natalie's shoulder. It was a lemur! "Is that tame enough for you, Miss Natalie?" laughed Hery.

Natalie's new friend was a common brown lemur. (I'd say a male, based on what it looked like between his legs!) It was greyish-brown with a black face and a long snout. He made low grunting noises, looking at my sister with orange eyes. "He is hungry," Tatiana said, removing her plastic bag of mango pieces.

Tatiana placed one in Natalie's open palm. Using its nimble fingers, the lemur snatched the piece of fruit. "That tickles!" squealed Natalie.

Dad managed to get a photo just before the lemur jumped to the ground. There was a rustling in the bushes, and several more of the lemurs dropped from branches to join Natalie's friend. "I hope there's enough fruit to go around," Mum said, always concerned with fairness.

At the Lemur Conservation Centre, we saw three other species of lemur.

In the trees was a group of six or seven red-ruffed lemurs. With thick, reddish-brown fur they had long black tails and black feet. Their black faces were encircled by a fringe of orangey-brown fur. They looked like clowns.

Later, we were lucky enough to see a northern sportive lemur. These lemurs are nocturnal and are rarely seen by tourists. This one was snoozing in a hole in the V-shaped vertical fork of a dead tree. Hery picked up a branch from the ground and tapped the tree's trunk. The grey-brown fuzzball with the black button nose opened his large, round eyes, looked around dozily and then went back to sleep.

The third species of lemur was the best: the sifika. They have thick silky fur, mostly white with a reddish-brown chest, legs and arms. Their heads are pure white, except for a circle of black around the eyes and snout; the strikingly dark feature is matched by a pair of small black ears.

Clinging to slender tree trunks, the sifakas would push off and sail through the air. Like a circus act, they leapt back and forth, from one tree to another. After doing this for a few minutes, one of them barked a short, sharp warning.

"Danger..." whispered Tatiana. "Probably a hawk."

The sifakas dropped to the ground. Standing upright, arms in the air, they moved in short sideways bounces, before disappearing into the safety of the dense forest.

Lemurs definitely were my new favourite animals.

"Tatiana, you have the best job in the world!" Natalie said.

"And she's brilliant at it," Hery said. "Intelligent, caring, creative— "

"You're embarrassing me, Hery, please stop," Tatiana protested. Then she added with a coaxing smile, "But first insert 'beautiful' to your list!" We stood in the car park ready to drive back to Tana. We had been asking Tatiana questions about her job helping Madagascar's animals.

"What has been your best day, Tatiana?" Natalie asked.

"Hmmm, my best day... I'm not really sure..."

"What about the tortoises?" suggested Hery.

"Yes, the radiated tortoises. My best day – and my worst day."

"What are radiated tortoises?" Mum asked.

"They're lovely," Tatiana said. "They have dark shells with patterns of yellow lines."

"Like a firework display," added Hery.

Tatiana explained that the tortoises were illegally hunted, another example of animals captured for the international pet market. A couple of years ago Tatiana worked for a veterinary doctor. One day the police called for medical assistance. Something had been found at a nearby house.

"When I arrived and saw what was there, I immediately burst into tears."

"In all the rooms," Hery said. "Wall-to-wall tortoises."

There were over five thousand of them! All waiting to be smuggled out of the country.

"The tortoises were starving," Tatiana said. "Some were too weak and did not make it."

"But you saved so many of them, Tatiana," Hery said to the young woman. Turning to us, he said, "She arranged for some to be looked after in conservation areas or zoos."

"A few were released into the wild," Tatiana added.

"That's an amazing story," Mum said.

"It sure is," Dad said. He looked at his watch. "One last question for Tatiana?"

Hayley put up her hand.

"Yes, Hayley?" said Tatiana.

Hayley looked from Hery to Tatiana. "If *he* asked you out on a date, would you say 'Yes'?"

Tatiana stroked her chin reflectively. "*Him*? On a date? Hmmm... I would have to think carefully about this... I mean he's not bad looking. A bit short and doesn't always brush his—"

"We have a long drive ahead of us," Hery interrupted, his light brown face taking on a hint of pink. "Time to go!"

A half-hour later, back on the main road, we were still teasing Hery.

"...And you can name your first three children Hayley, Brandon and Natalie."

"Good idea, Hayley," said Mum. "And the next two will be Julian and Alexandra."

"I think..." Hery said, suppressing a smile, "...that all of you can *walk* back to—"

There was a blur of yellow to our left as a car shot past. In this stupid attempt to overtake us, the driver forced an oncoming car to swerve into our lane. Hery turned the wheel hard, just managing to avoid the oncoming car.

Hery signalled and pulled over to the side of the road. He got out of the minivan. "*Adala!*" He yelled in the direction of the driver of the yellow car, which was now long gone.

Hery walked back up the road to the other car, which had also pulled over. He spoke with the driver for a minute then returned to the minivan.

"They're fine," he said, getting into the driver's seat.

"That was a close call," Dad said. "Thanks to Hery's great reflexes."

"Necessary to survive on Madagascar's roads. Is everybody all right?"

"I think so..." Mum said. "Children?"

"We're okay," Hayley said, speaking for the three of us. "Just a bit shaken up."

Hery started the minivan and we continued on our journey.

Hayley was right. I was a bit shaken up... and something else. I had a funny feeling. A weird and unpleasant feeling. I felt it when that yellow car whizzed past.

Chapter 8

Some Bad News

Tortoises have been on Earth for millions and millions of years. The Pinta giant tortoise lived on one of the Galapagos Islands, six hundred miles off the coast of South America. In the 1600s, hungry sailors from whaling ships stopped at the islands, and easily caught the slow-moving reptiles. The last Pinta giant tortoise, a male known as Lonesome George, died in 2012, age 101.

There is *another* Madagascar. *Not* the one on travel posters or in TV nature programmes. This Madagascar doesn't have white sandy beaches or smiling people performing traditional dances in colourful costumes. Here, there are no cute animals. For thirty million people – many of the people who call this island home – this was the *real* Madagascar: a land of hardship and poverty.

We saw glimpses of this other Madagascar through the minivan's windows as we drove back to our comfortable, clean hotel. Standing by the side of the road were groups of barefoot children, waving and calling out for money and sweets. Women filled up large yellow canisters at concrete water wells, which they then carried long distances to their dusty villages. Boys my age trudged through the knee-deep mud of rice fields, urging massive water buffaloes to pull their heavy ploughs.

The rice fields. They were everywhere! A vast jigsaw puzzle. Some pieces were brown, some yellow, but most were different hues of green.

"People sure grow a lot of rice in this country," observed Natalie.

"In my country when we invite people to a meal, we say *'Manasa hihinam-bary'* – which means *'Let's eat some rice!'"*

"I've cooked rice a thousand times, Hery," Mum said, "but I'm ashamed to say I know nothing about it."

"It's little bits of white stuff that you eat, Mum," I said. "There. Now you know something about it."

"Thank you, Brandon Wikipedia Fletcher," Mum said sarcastically, then spoke to Hery again. "I mean – how it gets from the ground to our kitchen table."

"Then Hery will teach you!" Hery pulled over to the side of the road. Sounding like a wise philosopher, he said, *To know a country, one must know its rice.*"

"Who said that?" Dad asked.

"Me. Just now!"

Laughing, we got out of the minivan, and stretched our arms and legs. (On this holiday we seemed to be spending more time in the minivan than out of it.)

Hery cleared his throat. "There are many different stages in the growing of rice. All happening at the same time in different fields. That way we are able to eat rice throughout the year."

"And that's why the fields are different colours?"

"Yes, Mr Fletcher. You are absolutely right." Hery pointed to some brown fields where many people were stooped over, close to the ground. "Growing rice is hard work. Those people are planting seeds by hand." Hery explained that rice needs loads of water, so the newly planted fields are then flooded.

He indicated another field, this one with tall, densely-packed, bright green grass. "The rice grows fast. Those tall plants will soon be picked and replanted so they have more room."

In another field, more people were bent over. "Every day the *weeds* must be picked." We learned that when the plants turn yellow, the stalks are cut down. The rice is removed by hand – then cleaned, bagged and sent to the supermarket.

"Thanks, Hery," Mum said.

Our lesson in rice-growing over, we continued the drive home.

Back at the hotel, we went to our rooms to rest. Hayley and Natalie played some silly card game involving a cat, rats and a piece of cheese. I took out my sketchbook and pencil. I wanted to be the first person in the universe to draw those newly-discovered lemurs. I flipped through the pack of postcards but couldn't find the one with 'Romeo' and 'Juliet'. I must have dropped it in the car. No problem. I picked my second choice – the indri – and started drawing...

A little later, we went downstairs to the hotel restaurant. This evening we had time to look at the framed photos on the walls.

"I want to see one of those," Mum said, pointing to the photo of a tree. Its smooth, thick trunk climbed high into the sky, topped by a surprisingly small clump of branches.

"A baobab," said Hayley. "Remember, Mum? From *The Little Prince*, that book you read us last winter."

The other photos included a ring-tailed lemur carrying a baby on its back; a scuba diver swimming with a green turtle; an old woman selling bundles of brown, pencil-length vanilla beans; and a multicoloured chameleon standing on a branch.

"Look, Brandon," Natalie said, pointing across the room at another photo. It showed a man about to throw a metal ball. On the ground in front of him were other metal balls and a little wooden one. "It's that game you played in France."

"Pétanque," I said. "I didn't know they played it here."

"In 2016, we were world champions!" The voice belonged to the hotel waiter. He showed us to a table and handed us menus. Mum and Dad ordered beef curry with spinach. My sisters and I decided on the Margherita pizzas.

"I have an idea," Mum said, as we waited for our meal.

"No, Mum," Hayley groaned. "Not one of your silly word games."

"Not this time," Mum said cheerfully. "A competition: who can fold a table napkin into the most interesting shape."

"We know who's going to win *this* challenge," Dad said.

"Dad, you never win anything!" I said.

"It's true – I *have* had a run of bad luck in family contests," Dad admitted, picking up the white napkin in front of him. "But this time the trophy goes to me!"

The competition began. The thick, cloth napkins bent easily, yet also held their shape.

Five minutes later, Mum called time. "Let's see everyone's masterpiece!"

Mum's flower was quite realistic, though a bit floppy. Natalie's unicorn was okay, though she needed to use the straw from her Coke for the horn. Dad made something that was *supposed* to be The Statue of Liberty but looked more like an ice cream cone that had been left in the sun too long. Hayley ended the game by holding up a crumpled napkin. *"Ta-dah!* Behold The Crumpled Napkin!" and proclaimed herself the winner. In the end, Mum said Natalie's was the best, but that was only because she wouldn't let me use ketchup for my erupting volcano.

After the main meal, we had dessert – vanilla-flavoured banana cake – and then headed back to our rooms.

"Look, everyone," Natalie said, as we walked past the bar. "We're on the telly!"

The television was showing the news. Dressed smartly, a man and a woman stood behind a newsreader's desk. On the back wall behind them was a massive photo: an enlargement of Tatiana's shot of us with the new lemurs.

"Uh-oh," Mum said, listening to the French-speaking newsreaders. (She had done most of the talking on our holiday in the south of France.)

"What, Mum?" I asked. "What's wrong?"

"Romeo and Juliet – they've been stolen!"

The news story ended. We went upstairs, gathering in Mum and Dad's room. All talk was about the kidnapped lemurs.

"It must have happened right after we saw them."

"Who could have done such a horrible thing?"

"Where are they keeping them?"

I stayed out of the conversation, busy with my own thoughts. *A strange man gives me a postcard showing two lemurs – lemurs unknown to the world. Then the lemurs are discovered. The postcard goes missing – and so do the lemurs.*

What was going on here?

Chapter 9

The İncident at the Ancient Fort

Baobab trees can grow up to thirty metres tall and live for two-thousand years. This iconic plant of Madagascar not only offers stunning photo opportunities, but its fruit is flavourful and nutritious. Three of Madagascar's six species face extinction due to the world's rising temperatures – caused by man-made climate change.

In the minivan the next morning, I looked for the missing postcard. I couldn't find it. Maybe its disappearance had nothing to do with the abducted lemurs. Yet maybe it did. Either way, I didn't share my suspicions with the others.

Hery had also seen last night's news. He was angry too. He told us that the criminals would try to get the animals out of the country to sell to rich buyers.

"Can't the police stop them?" asked Hayley.

"It is not easy smuggling animals out of an island country like Madagascar. But these criminals are clever. They wait for the right time and the right place."

Hery didn't think there was much hope that the lemurs would ever be found.

"*Anjara*," Hery said. "It is something we cannot change. I don't know the word in English."

"Fate," Mum said.

"I like *anjara* better," said Natalie. "*Anjara!*"

As we drove away from Tana on our way to some famous fort, Hery taught us other words and phrases in Malagasy. His short lesson included how to say, "What's your name?" and "Thank you." We even learned the word that he occasionally shouted at other drivers: *Adala!* That meant *Idiot!*

"Wow, sixteen million eggs!" exclaimed Natalie.

We stood outside the high stone wall of a 300-year-old wooden fort. Hery had just explained how the wall had been constructed from concrete made from sand, shells and the whites of sixteen million chicken eggs.

Hery indicated a rectangular opening in the wall. "This is one of the four entrances to the palace compound – the South Gate. There is the South Gate, the East Gate, the North Gate and—"

"The West Gate!" Dad called out.

"Yay, Dad," Hayley said, slowly clapping her hands with exaggerated praise.

Hery smiled, then continued. "Does anyone see anything interesting about this entrance?"

We looked for several moments. Then I saw it. Or to be precise, I *didn't* see it.

"There's no door."

"Well done, Mr Brandon." Hery pointed to the left. Leaning against the wall was a massive stone slab, like the gravestone of a beanstalk giant. "When the Merina people – the Malagasy tribe that *I* belong to – were under attack from other tribes, this stone would be dragged to block the entranceway. It took forty slaves to move it."

"Slaves?" Natalie blinked. "But I didn't know that – I mean I thought that... slaves were kept by—"

"...only white people?" Hery smiled grimly. "Cruel human beings come in all colours... Come, let us go inside." Hery led us through the rectangular gateway.

There wasn't a whole lot to see inside the walls of the fort. Scattered around the dusty grounds were small, wooden huts. There was a royal palace, but it was really just a bigger hut, not like the luxurious marble buildings we saw in India.

The king lived here – with his many wives. And he made some ridiculous rules. For example, when visiting him, you had to enter the building with your right foot first. When leaving, you began with your left foot – and had to walk backwards!

Near the top of the ceiling of this high-roofed structure, there was a wooden platform. When a visitor entered the room, the king would hide up there in the dark, with small pebbles in his hand. If the king did not want to meet with the caller, he would drop the pebbles to the floor. That was the signal for his wife to say that her husband wasn't home.

When we left the building, we all tried walking backwards, starting with the left foot. It wasn't difficult, it just felt stupid. A stupid rule from a king who sat in the top of his palace throwing rocks. A king who had only one bath a year!

After visiting the royal palace, we climbed to the top of a stone watchtower for a view of the surrounding countryside, which was flat and tree-less. Here, one of the king's soldiers would have been able to see for miles in every direction. "If he spotted an enemy army coming, he would call for help," Hery said.

"On his iPhone?" asked Hayley.

Natalie giggled.

"No, Miss Hayley," Hery removed something that was hanging on the watchtower wall. "On this."

"A zebu horn," Dad said.

"Right, Mr Fletcher."

"What's a zebu?" Natalie asked.

"Remember, Natalie?" I said. "Those cows crossing the road today." Similar to the cattle we saw in India, zebus had humped backs and large curving horns.

"Can I try the horn, Hery?" I asked.

Hery smiled. "This one is sacred, Mr Brandon. Even I am not allowed to blow it." Hanging the horn back up on the wall, he added, "You will have to buy your *own* horn at a souvenir shop."

We exited the fort through the North Gate. Along the outside of the wall, Malagasy people were selling all sorts of arts and crafts: colourful baskets made from the fibres of palm trees; African masks, the wooden faces expressive with royal power; painted wood chameleons; Madagascar-themed mobile phone accessories; T-shirts with pictures of Malagasy animals; tiny models of bicycles made from scraps of aluminium, electrical wires and hospital rubber tubing.

I was the only one in the family who didn't buy anything. Natalie found a T-shirt with a picture of Madagascar's extinct elephant bird. Hayley bought herself a phone case covered in cartoon ring-tailed lemurs. Dad, who collects coffee mugs, found one with a bright green chameleon.

We reached the last souvenir seller, where tourists crowded around a long table filled with items carved from the zebu horns: drinking mugs, miniature baobab trees, animal figurines, jewellery, kitchen utensils – and blowing horns like the one used by the watchtower soldier in the fort. Mum picked out two sets of salad servers, one for her and one for Nan. I had my eyes on a zebu blowing horn – a polished white one with black speckles –

but when I found out the high price, I decided to give it a miss.

It was time to go. As we joined the flow of tourists back to the car park, I became separated from the others. A hand touched my shoulder. Expecting Mum or Dad, I turned around – and gasped in surprise. It was the man with the red eyes! He smiled at me, his dark face above the white beard crinkling into countless fine lines.

"What? What do you want?" My words were an equal mixture of curiosity and fear.

Instead of answering he gently pushed a medium-sized package into my hands, smiled that sad, pleading smile of his and walked away. I tried following him with my eyes, but he had disappeared into the crowd.

I held up the package. It was curved and wrapped in birthday-like wrapping paper, covered with a pattern: simple pictures of a brown and white zebu.

I felt another hand on my shoulder. I tensed up, afraid. With effort, I slowly turned my head...

...And there was Dad! I breathed a sigh of relief.

"Here you are, Brandon. C'mon. Everybody's waiting."

Discreetly shifting the package behind my back, I took Dad's hand. As we walked towards the others, Dad didn't seem to notice that I was shaking a bit. Partially from having another encounter with that strange man – but mostly from excitement; I couldn't wait to find out what was inside the mystery package.

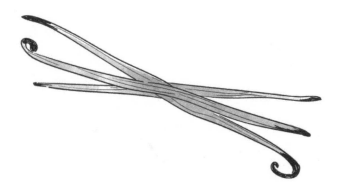

Chapter 10
The Funny Feeling Returns

Standing three metres tall, Madagascar's elephant bird laid an egg that weighed ten kilograms, the same weight as one hundred and sixty chicken eggs. It was the largest bird that ever lived, surviving on Earth for millions of years. Bad luck arrived one thousand years ago when seafaring people reached the island and hunted the flightless birds for their meat. Rats from the boats ate the birds' eggs. Extinction quickly followed.

"Some guy *gave* it to you?"

"For the fourth time, Hayley – yes!"

We sat at a circular table by our hotel's small swimming pool. I had just recounted what had happened at the souvenir market.

I left out the fact that it was the same old man from the other night. I'm not sure why. Maybe because Mum might get upset, thinking some weirdo was following her precious son. Or maybe it was because I somehow felt *connected* to the old man. In a strange way, the connection was special, and I didn't feel like sharing it.

On the table was the mysterious package.

"Open it, Brandon!" Natalie begged, pushing the package towards me.

I picked it up, surprised at its lightness. Crescent-shaped, it was about half a metre long.

I tore off the zebu-patterned paper to discover... a blowing horn. It was white with black speckles, polished smooth.

"That's the one I saw at the souvenir stall," I said. "The expensive one. The one I liked."

"Isn't that strange..." Mum said.

"Give it a go, Brandon," Dad said.

I held the horn to my lips and blew. Nothing. Just the pressurised squawk of my breath. I tried again with the same result.

"You'll need to practise," Dad said.

"Can I try?" asked Hayley.

"Are you a Merina warrior, entrusted by the spirits of Malagasy ancestors to protect the king?"

"What? What are you talking about, Brandon?"

"Just as I figured." I put the horn in my rucksack.

*   *   *

"Water lily," Mum said.

Another day. Another adventure. Another one of Mum's language games: words with 'water' in them.

"I will say... water *buffalo*." Hery pointed to a rice field where the muscular animal dragged a plough through the mud.

"How about... watercolours," Dad said.

"You mean like that painting of yours, Dad?" I asked, putting the new horn back in my rucksack (after again failing to produce a sound).

Last summer Dad had taken a watercolour class. We all teased him about *Midnight in the Arctic*.

"You are a painter, Mr Fletcher?"

"Just a beginner, Hery. But I think you would have loved this painting. It was like... like standing under the Northern Lights at the top of the world."

"Just watch out for that killer lamb standing on the iceberg!" Hayley advised.

"It was a *polar bear*," Dad said to Hery. And melodramatically added (to the entire universe), "Another great artist unappreciated in his own lifetime!"

"Sure, Dad," I said dismissively. "Your turn, Natalie. Another water word, please."

"Okay. I say... hey, what's *that* place?" We drove past a modern-looking, three-storey brick building sticking out in the middle of the flat countryside.

"That is the National Seed Bank, Miss Natalie. In that building, there are seeds from all over Madagascar. From every type of plant."

"Even orchids?"

"Especially orchids, Mrs Fletcher. Just yesterday, my brother wrote a news story about a recently discovered orchid. A beautiful purple one. A few seeds from this plant were immediately sent to the scientists in that building to be safely locked away."

"Does that mean they have vanilla seeds there?" I asked.

"Who'd want to keep stupid old vanilla seeds?"

"Hayley, what do you have against vanilla?"

"It's lame, Mum." Hayley again reminded us that she wasn't too keen on today's visit to a vanilla plantation.

"Hayley, you might enjoy it," said the always positive Natalie.

"What? Enjoy a boring old tour guide giving us boring old information about a boring old ice cream flavour?"

"Boring, Hayley?" Dad said. "According to last year's survey, vanilla is the number one ice cream in the UK. Followed by mint chocolate chip and then chocolate."

"You know much about ice cream flavours, Mister Fletcher."

"He's on a pub quiz team, Hery," Mum said, "with some of his workmates."

"They drink beer and show off their knowledge of meaningless facts," Hayley said.

"Meaningless? You mean *fascinating*, don't you? Longest river in the world: the Amazon at 6,800 kilometres. Top-selling car in the UK: the Ford Fiesta. Favourite emoji: face with tears of joy. Most popular dog in the UK: either Labrador Retriever or French Bulldog, depending on where you live. Most—"

"Irritating father in the whole universe," Hayley interrupted. "Mr Julian Fletcher!"

Dad ignored our mock cheering and asked Hery which ice cream flavour *he* liked.

"Like the colour of my skin – I am a chocolate man! And the Fletchers? Your favourites?"

"I like bubble gum," Hayley said. "Mum goes for salted caramel, Dad always gets coffee, Natalie can't live without her coconut – and if an ice cream shop doesn't have mint chocolate chip, Brandon gets hysterical."

"Mr Brandon gets *hysterical*?" asked Hery with his cheeky smile. "I do not know that flavour!"

Hery was a funny guy.

"We are almost there," said Hery. The dusty track climbed uphill, ending at an old two-storied wooden house. Hery parked the minivan in front of the building in an empty dirt car park.

"Mum, Dad..." Hayley groaned. "I'm not really sure I'm up for this. This morning I bumped my leg on the bed and it still hurts. Also, I think I'm getting a headache. *Plus,* whenever I move my neck—"

"We get the message, Hayley," Mum said. (The message being, 'I'm going to be miserable on this tour and will make it miserable for everyone else.') Mum glanced at Dad questioningly.

"I suppose... that she'd be okay," Dad said.

"Thanks, Dad! Thanks, Mum! I'll keep the door locked."

That settled, the rest of us got out of the minivan. The front door of the house opened. A figure emerged and started walking towards us. A young man. Younger-looking than Hery, he was slim with light-brown skin. He wore a green and white football shirt and faded blue jeans.

"Is he in a boy band?" Natalie whispered.

Mum smiled, nodding her head in agreement. "He's cute, isn't he?"

The young man reached us. "Hello, my name is Elino. And you must be the famous Fletcher family."

"I'm Julian," Dad said, shaking hands with Elino. "My wife Alex. And this is Brandon and Natalie."

"Who is going to bombard you with millions of questions," I added.

"Well, I hope I will be ready with millions of answers. Please. Come with me." We began following Elino up the hill that ran alongside the house.

From behind, there was the sound of a minivan's door violently sliding open and the thudding clang as it slammed shut.

"Hey! What about me!"

Hayley was sprinting towards us. We stopped to wait for her.

"And this..." Dad said to Elino, "...is Hayley. She doesn't like vanilla."

"But she *loves* boys," I whispered to her.

"Maybe by the end of the tour she will change her mind," said Elino. "Please. Come this way."

"Your shoes, Brandon."

"What, Mum? Oh, yeah." These new trainers. The laces kept coming undone. "You go ahead, I'll be right there." The others continued walking up the hill and I bent over to tie my shoes.

That's when the funny feeling came back. The same one I had when we were nearly run off the road.

I stood up, looking back down the hill where the road threaded through the rice fields. In the distance, parked alongside the road, was a yellow car. And now I could make out two figures – backs to me, facing roadside bushes, legs spread apart. Obviously, men. One much taller than the other one.

The men finished what they were doing. They got in the yellow car and drove away. When the car disappeared into the distance, so did the funny feeling.

Chapter 11
Another Robbery

The Arctic is home to the polar bear, the world's largest land animal. Survivors for hundreds of thousands of years, polar bears now feel the effects of human-caused global warming. With less food available many adult bears and their cubs have perished. As the population decreases, the very existence of these magnificent creatures is threatened.

"Thinking of becoming a rice farmer, Brandon?"

It was Dad. He had joined me in overlooking the countryside below.

"I don't think so, Dad," I laughed. "Don't want to work that hard."

"Yeah, I know what you mean," he said. "Maybe growing vanilla is easier." Dad motioned me to come along and together we started after the others.

Like most enjoyable activities, the two-hour tour went by really quickly. I think even Hayley found it interesting.

The tour had begun with a visit to countless rows of trees, grown as 'posts' for the vanilla plants. The long vines, with their large leaves, wrapped themselves around the trees' trunks or dangled from their branches.

Elino showed us the green buds that would one day open into yellow flowers. Vanilla flowers had to be pollinated by hand (because Madagascar didn't have the right kind of insects or birds that pollinate vanilla plants in other parts of the world). This human pollination required great care and took loads of time. That was one of the reasons why vanilla was so expensive.

Vanilla farmers picked the growing beans when they were green and bitter-tasting. Left out in the hot sun, they turned black. They now smelled of vanilla and were ready to travel to London where they would end up in Nan's famous cookies.

After the tour, we stopped at the small shop inside the house. Mum was the only one who had bought anything: for Nan, a jar of vanilla powder and two vacuum-sealed packs of the actual beans; for herself, a large bottle of liquid vanilla extract.

"For me, the most interesting part was finding out that vanilla plants are members of the orchid family."

Back in the minivan, Mum started off by sharing her favourite part of the tour. Dad hadn't known that vanilla originally came from Mexico, where the plants were pollinated by hummingbirds. I was surprised that there were one hundred and fifty types of vanilla plants – but only fifteen of them made the vanilla flavour. Natalie couldn't believe that the vanilla flower blooms for only one day a year.

"What about you, Hayley," Natalie asked, "What was *your* favourite part?"

"That's easy," I said. "When she tripped and Elino caught her in his arms!"

"Yes, good ploy, Hayley," Dad said.

"I *didn't* do it on purpose!"

"You did so!" I countered.

"Did not!"

"Did so!"

"I DID NOT!"

"Enough already!" Dad shouted.

"Yes, Dad," Hayley and I said, and we were silent.

Hery, looking in the rear-view mirror, was the only one who noticed me mouth, "Did so." I saw the faint hint of a smile as we continued the long drive home.

*　　*　　*

"Can you *describe* these feelings, Bran?"

"Just feelings, Mum. It's hard to explain." As we finished breakfast the following day, I tried to talk about what I'd experienced yesterday at the vanilla plantation.

"And it happens when you see *yellow cars*?"

"Not *all* yellow cars, Hayley. Just the one near the lemur centre and the one down by the side of the road."

"Which might or might not be the same car," Dad added.

There was a short silence, broken by Mum. "Seems like some odd things are happening to you on this trip, Bran. The man with the postcards, that horn someone gave you, the funny feelings..."

"Odd things are *always* happening to Brandon when we go on holiday," Natalie said.

Natalie was talking about Turkey, India and France. There the mysteries at least made some kind of sense. Each was a *single picture*, a puzzle just waiting for the different pieces to be put together.

But what was going on here in Madagascar? An old man with red eyes. A postcard. Kidnapped animals. A yellow car.

Buried in my own thoughts, I was only half-listening to the family conversation.

"Well, I think if it happens again, we should find a doctor and..." Mum stopped mid-sentence.

"What is it, Alex?" Dad asked.

"Look. On the television." Mum pointed towards the bar. It was the news again. A young woman stood behind her desk. Across the screen behind her was a large headline: "*Vol à la Banque Nationale de Semences.*"

"What does it say, Mum?" Natalie asked.

"It says... *'Robbery at National Seed Bank!'*"

Appearing behind the newsreader was a large photo: a photo of a beautiful purple flower. This picture was followed by one of a three-storey, brick building.

"That seed bank!" Haley said. "The one Hery showed us yesterday."

"Somebody call my name?" At that moment, a smiling Hery showed up. "Good morning, Fletchers. Are you ready to—"

"Hery, that place with all the seeds," Natalie said. "It's been robbed!"

Hery strode over to the bar and returned a few minutes later. "You are right. Many seeds have been stolen, including those belonging to the new orchid."

"But why would anybody steal *seeds*?"

"To sell to rich people, Mum," Hayley said. "So they can show off their precious flowers to all their stupid rich friends."

"Miss Hayley is right."

"Hery, did the news say if the police had any leads?" Dad asked.

"I'm afraid not," Hery said. "No, I am wrong, Mr Fletcher. There *was* one clue. From a security camera."

"What was it?" I asked. I had a pretty good idea what Hery's answer would be.

"A car. Parked near the building around midnight. A yellow car."

Everybody in my family turned to look at me.

"Brandon," Natalie said. "That's *your* car."

Chapter 12

They Better Not Touch Mimi!

Hummingbirds live in North, Central and South America, and on islands in the Caribbean. The sight of one of these colourful birds extracting nectar from a flower with its needle-like bill is a magical experience. Of the 300 species of hummingbird, over thirty are threatened with extinction. This is due to climate change and the destruction of their habitat.

"You own a *car*?" Hery asked incredulously.

"No, it's just that..."

"The other day, when you took us to the lemur park, Brandon had a funny feeling when he saw a yellow car and then we found out that those new lemurs had been stolen and then, yesterday, Brandon had another funny feeling when he saw another yellow car and then we just found out that those seeds had been stolen by someone in a yellow car so he thinks the funny feelings and the yellow cars and the lemur-nappings and the seed-nappings somehow go together!"

Natalie could sure talk fast!

Dad removed his glasses, wiping them on his shirt before putting them back on. "I think... for now... we need to separate what Brandon was feeling... and what has actually happened. All we know is that criminals are stealing rare plants and animals."

Hery explained that thieves like this – or their bosses – need to find ways to get their stolen goods out of the country. That wouldn't be a problem with the seeds, which are small and easy to hide. Getting the *lemurs* past border control was a much bigger problem. But as Hery had said earlier, the criminals only had to wait – for the right place and the right time.

"The big question is," said Hayley, "will they strike again?

*   *   *

"I feel like I'm glued to this seat!" Hayley, like the rest of us, had been sitting too long in the minivan.

For today's outing, we again drove far from the city, deep into the countryside. Now, leaving behind the villages and neatly cultivated rice fields, we were climbing into the rugged hills.

Hery pointed into the distance at a small patch of green. "See those trees? That's where we're going."

The patch of green grew larger until we found ourselves at another animal protection area: PHILIBERT'S REPTILE RESERVE. We parked, got out of the minivan and stretched our legs. We followed Hery through a gate in the reserve's metal perimeter fence.

Inside, near a small wooden building, was a rickety plastic table and chair. An old man, dressed in a brown park ranger uniform, sat there gently snoring. Without waking the old man, Hery quietly put some money in a metal box that was on the table and motioned for us to follow him.

Scattered among the trees were cages – some similar to rabbit hutches, others more like small zoo enclosures. This place was another refuge for animals needing care and protection. It was the same situation as with the lemurs. Many of these reptiles had been kept as pets and neglected by their owners; others were found in the wild, hungry or sick; a few, like Tatiana's tortoises, had been rescued from animal smugglers and brought here for safety.

"Look, Zecko!" Natalie said, pulling her hand puppet out of her rucksack. "Some new friends for you!"

"G-g-g-geckos!"

In the first cages we visited there were lizards, starting with the geckos. All sorts of geckos, ranging in size from about 10 – 40 centimetres . Bright green geckos with red markings. Geckos that looked like dry brown leaves. Grey-white geckos clinging to the trunks of trees, camouflaged against the pale mottled bark.

Next came the chameleons, similar in size to the geckos, and just as interesting. There was a lance-nosed chameleon with a long, thin snout resembling the horn of a narwhal; a leaf chameleon with a flat brown body that perfectly blended in with dry leaves that had fallen to the ground; a jewelled chameleon, its green body covered in rows of brightly-coloured, pearl-like dots.

Living in a large cage built around a tree was the largest chameleon in the world, a Parson's chameleon. This one, over a half a metre long, was blue with black stripes and a tightly curled tail. We watched with fascination as it crawled along a branch, stalking his next meal, a small brown grasshopper. Slowly, almost imperceptibly, the chameleon moved towards the unsuspecting insect... Then – zap! A tongue shot out like a whip – and the grasshopper ended up in the chameleon's mouth. You could hear muffled crunching sounds as the sleepy-eyed reptile enjoyed his meal. All of the grasshopper – head, body, wings and long skinny legs.

"Disgusting," said Hayley. (Hayley liked *most* disgusting things, but not ones that might end up in her mouth.)

"*Disgusting*, Hayley?" said Dad. "Insects are the food of the future."

"They're not in my future."

"Think of the *tempting choices*," Dad continued. "Beetle burgers, cricket crumble, ladybird lasagne, butterfly flapjacks, bumble bee—"

"Not *butterflies*," protested Natalie. Butterflies were one of my younger sister's (many) favourite creatures. She had a colourful poster in her room with European butterflies and moths.

"Many Malagasy people eat insects, Miss Hayley," Hery said. "It is that – or starvation."

"Have you eaten them, Hery?" Mum asked.

"Yes, my mother makes delicious, deep-fried locusts. I will get the recipe for you! But now I would like to show you something very special." Hery led us to another small hutch with sides made from chicken wire. He opened the wooden door and reached inside. From among the leaves and twigs, he gently removed something and held his cupped hands out towards us. "Voila!" he said, taking away one of his hands.

There was a chorus of "wows" (and an "OMG" from Hayley).

On Hery's thumbnail was a tiny brown lizard.

"A baby chameleon!" exclaimed Natalie.

"No, Miss Natalie."

"No? Is it a gecko?"

"You are right about it being a chameleon." Hery smiled knowingly. "How old are you, Miss Natalie?"

"Eight."

Hery pointed at the tiny creature. "She is not a baby. You two are the same age."

"Are you kidding us, Hery?"

"I would not do that, Miss Hayley. This chameleon is fully grown. Her scientific name is *Brookesia Micra*. But here at the centre, they call her Mimi."

Hery had saved the best cage for last. Each of us had a go holding Mimi. When it was Dad's turn, he let me take a photo of him and the smallest chameleon in the world.

Our visit over, we started heading back to the park exit. "Those bad men who stole the lemurs," Hayley said fiercely, "They better not touch Mimi!"

"How do you know they're men?" Mum challenged.

Natalie joined in. "Yeah, Hayley, there are loads of female baddies. There's the White Witch in Narnia."

"And Bellatrix Lestrange from the Harry Potter books," Mum added. "Mrs Coulter in *His Dark Materials*. The Other Mother in *Coraline*, and Mrs—"

"Okay, okay already!" Hayley said. "I stand corrected. I was just saying that only a *man* could kidnap *poor defenceless animals*."

"What about Cruella De Vil?" Dad said, a sucker for old Walt Disney films.

"Good one, Mr Fletcher!" said Hery. "My brother and I have watched *The 101 Dalmatians* many times!"

Hery's brother? An idea popped into my head. "Hery. Your brother – he works for a newspaper, right?"

"Yes, Mr Brandon. Why do you ask?"

"Er, no reason, really. Just thinking about something."

A plan was forming. A plan that could save the lemurs.

Chapter 13
The Six-Point Plan

Every autumn, Monarch butterflies migrate from Canada to Mexico, a three-thousand-mile flight. Not so long ago, ten million of these orange, black and white insects could be found in a small forest near Mexico City. That number has now dropped to thirty thousand. Climate change and farmers' pesticides could result in the Monarch's extinction.

Back in Tana, we stopped at an Italian restaurant for a late lunch. While we waited for our pizzas, I explained my plan.

Mum wasn't convinced. "I just don't know..." she said, her arms crossed, each hand undecidedly rubbing the opposite upper arm. "You *know* I don't believe in telling lies."

"How about Nan's hat?" Hayley asked.

Good one, Hayley! Last week Nan bought a new beanie. It was yellow with a green pom-pom on top. It looked like she was wearing a pineapple on her head.

"You hated it, but you said it was lovely."

Mum's face flushed with embarrassment. "No, Hayley, I mean that was – you know – I didn't want to hurt her feelings. That was – that was different."

"Consider it this way, Alex," suggested Dad. "A bit of harmless dishonesty... in exchange for a chance to save those lemurs."

What a clever dad! He takes two of Mum's sacred beliefs and drops them into the wrestling ring. Tonight's Main Event – *Telling the Truth* v *Concern for Living things.*"

"What do you think, Mum?" I asked.

And the winner is...

Mum repeatedly clapped her cheeks with both hands. "Well... I suppose... in this situation... it might be okay – just once – to tell a little white lie."

BRANDON ABROAD: THE MISSING LEMURS

And the winner is... Concern for Living Things! My idea had Mum's approval.

I took out my sketchbook. "I propose a 6-Point plan."

1. *An article is planted in the newspaper announcing the discovery of a new animal.*
2. *The thieves read about the animal.*
3. *They attempt to kidnap it.*
4. *They get caught by the police.*
5. *They confess to the other crimes, disclosing the location of the abducted lemurs.*
6. *Romeo and Juliet are rescued!*

"Hery, do you think your brother will agree to help out?" Dad asked.

"I <u>know</u> that he will," Hery said with a smile. "I am bigger than he is!"

We rested in our rooms for a couple of hours before going out again. In the growing darkness outside the hotel, Hery was waiting for us.

"What did your brother say?" I blurted out impatiently. I heard Mum clearing her throat. Oh, right. Manners. "Hello, Hery?" I said with exaggerated sweetness. "I hope you had a pleasant afternoon. WHAT DID YOUR BROTHER SAY?"

Hery smiled broadly, giving the 'thumbs up' of success. "It will be in tomorrow morning's newspaper."

There was cheering all around. Then we piled into the minivan. Hery was taking us on a night-time adventure.

Twenty minutes later, we were far from the lights of the city. We drove along a seemingly endless straight road, bordered by trees, their tall black silhouettes just visible against the dark sky. Hery signalled and pulled off to the side of the road and parked.

"Here we are," Hery said.

"Wait, children," Mum urged.

A pair of headlights pierced the darkness. A massive lorry. Only after it had rumbled past did we get out of the minivan. We stood around in the dark, waiting for further instructions. Hery removed a large torch from his rucksack and switched it on. Then he produced smaller torches and gave one to each of us. "Come. The creatures of the night are waiting."

"Will we see an aye-aye?" I asked, switching on my torch.

"Yes," said Natalie excitedly. "I want to see *Maurice*!"

"Who?" Dad asked. We explained to our ignorant father that Maurice was a character in the *Madagascar* film, the aye-aye with the deep voice. It was the bat-faced lemur on one my postcards, the nocturnal one with the long middle finger.

"I'm sorry, Miss Natalie, but we probably won't see an aye-aye. They are very shy." Hery explained that the aye-aye was endangered for many reasons. "Some of my people try to kill aye-ayes. They think this lemur is a sign of bad luck."

"Aye-ayes probably think *humans* are a sign of bad luck," I said, trying to sound wise.

"You must be right, Mr Brandon. They seem to avoid us at all costs, living high in the trees and only coming out at night."

In the criss-crossing beams of six torchlights, we now saw that between the road and the tall trees, also going on forever in both directions, was a metal fence. Hery opened a gate in the fence and we followed him inside. We were going on a night-time safari.

The forest was dark, the blackness of the hobbit's Mirkwood, where Bilbo Baggins and his friends became hopelessly lost. Here it also seemed a bit scary. But knowing that Hery was our leader made me feel fearless.

The jerkily moving light from the torches helped a little, keeping us on the rough narrow path we were following. Extra concentration was necessary to avoid tripping up on the occasional tree root or protruding rock.

It was a quiet darkness. No animal calls, no rustling in the bushes. Only footsteps on damp leaves and the sound of my own breathing.

Hery stopped suddenly. He aimed the beam of his torch at a nearby tree.

"Do you see it?" Hery asked in a hushed voice.

"What?" whispered Hayley. "A leaf?"

"Yes, but what else?" said Hery.

"Oh, *I* see it!" said Natalie.

I did too. On the branch was a green insect. Its body, encased in leaf-shaped wings, was supported by six incredibly skinny legs. The antennae were longer than the rest of its body!

"A katydid," Hery said.

We watched the motionless insect for a few minutes. Then Dad took a photo and we continued our walk.

From time to time Hery would stop to show us other creatures, including a blue-yellow frog, a bright green chameleon, a mouse lemur, a satanic leaf-tailed gecko and a red owl. In that hour-long tour, the only sounds made by our family were "Wow!" and "Amazing!" and "Take a picture, Dad!"

I felt so lucky to be here and have the chance to see these animals. Not in a book, not on telly, but in real life.

"Thanks, Hery," Dad said as we drove back to our hotel. "That was a real treat."

"Then you are not disappointed?" asked Hery.

"Disappointed?" Mum asked, surprised.

"Yes, we did not see an aye-aye."

"That's okay, Hery," Natalie said. "I've seen the film four times."

"I bet the aye-aye saw *us*," Hayley said. "In the dark, high up in the trees. Maybe even a whole family of them. Just sitting there, watching us."

I hope that Hayley was right. That we didn't see any because they were out of sight. Not because there weren't any around. It would be sad if aye-

ayes became extinct, and you could only see them in some silly cartoon.

Mum failed to suppress a loud yawn. "Excuse me," she said. "I'm ready for bed."

I was too. Not that I was very tired. I just couldn't wait to get through the night and see tomorrow morning's newspaper.

Chapter 14

Arson!

Like a woodpecker, the aye-aye taps on trees to find insects. After locating one, this small nocturnal lemur gnaws a hole in the wood and extracts the unlucky bug with its long thin middle finger. Considered by some people to be a sign of bad luck, aye-ayes are sometimes killed by superstitious farmers. This, along with the destruction of their forest habitat, is leading these shy creatures closer and closer to extinction.

"Brandon Fletcher! In *this* family, we don't use that sort of language."

"Sorry, Mum. But this is so *frustrating*." It was the morning after our magical night walk through the forest. As we sat in the hotel lobby, I repeatedly tried to get something out of that horn. A bad word had slipped from my mouth after yet another failure.

"Keep trying, son," Dad encouraged. "When I was a little boy—"

"Here comes Hery!" Hayley said.

"Good morning, Fletcher family! Including Brandon with his zebu horn. Have you made any sounds yet?"

"Only swear words," Natalie giggled.

"Do you mind if *I* try?" Hery asked.

I handed him the horn. Holding it in both hands, he blew and made a loud trumpety sound." He waved an apology to the startled young woman behind the check-in desk.

"How did you *do* that?" I asked, impressed and jealous.

"It's hard to explain," Hery said. "It's like... it's like you must *be the horn*."

"*Be the horn*?"

"Yes. I will show you later. But right now... I have something very important to share with you."

As I put the horn back in my rucksack, Hery produced a newspaper from behind his back. "Page four, Mr Brandon," he said, handing me the paper.

I turned to page four... and there it was.

"Read it, dear," Mum said.

I cleared my throat and began reading.

BACK FROM THE DEAD! – CHAMELEON REDISCOVERED

Scientists have discovered a family of Chamaeleon Fletcheratus, the Lemon-Lime Chameleon. Thought to have gone extinct in the 1990s, an adult male and female, along with three juveniles, were discovered two days ago in Zahamena National Park. These beautiful reptiles – with black bodies and alternating rows of yellow and green spots – are currently at the Philibert Reptile Reserve awaiting medical tests. They will soon be available for public viewing.

"'*Chamaeleon Fletcheratus*'," Hayley said. "We're famous!"

"Even *I* believe the story," Mum said, laughing.

"The park has agreed to the plan," said Hery. "And the police will be there. Now, all we need to do is wait."

Usually, I get very impatient when I have to wait for something. But not here in Madagascar. There are too many amazing creatures to distract me. Today, it was the ones that fly.

Back in the minivan, we were heading for a nearby bird sanctuary.

"What kinds of birds do you have in *London*?" Hery asked.

"In London?" Hayley said. "Pigeons. Boring grey pigeons. They're everywhere."

"If there weren't so many, Miss Hayley, then perhaps they would be less boring."

I hadn't thought of that before. But Hery was right. If pigeons were rare like the lemurs, we'd appreciate them more: their funny walk with the changes in direction and bobbing heads; the cooing sounds they make; the shiny, pink-green colouration on their necks; or the patterns on their wings.

"London has other birds too, Hery," Mum said. "In our garden, we get sparrows, robins, blackbirds, tits, goldfinches, and even the occasional woodpecker."

"Have you seen a painted stork, Hery?"

"No, Miss Natalie. Have you seen one?"

"Yes. On another holiday."

We told Hery about last February's experience at an Indian wetlands centre. Seeing all those exotic birds had motivated me to start saving money for a really good pair of binoculars.

The birds we saw today were also amazing. During the two-hour session – with the help of our young guide Patrick – we spotted twenty-three different species. I listed the sightings in my sketchbook, putting a star by my favourites. The starred ones included the (blue) coua, (orange) pygmy kingfisher, (brown and white) paradise flycatcher, (black and green) velvet asity and the (red) fody. Birds sure know how to do colours!

Lemurs were still my favourite animals. But birds were a close second. And while lemurs could only be found on an island in the Indian Ocean, birds were everywhere! After this bird-watching experience, I decided to become an ornithologist. As a professional birdwatcher, I would go all over the planet, taking photos of every single kind of bird – toucans, flamingos, hummingbirds, eagles, penguins – you name it. And on the front of my bestselling book would be a picture of a beautiful London pigeon.

Driving back from bird-watching, we glimpsed another part of everyday Malagasy life. We were crossing a concrete bridge that spanned a wide and mainly dry riverbed. The rainy season hadn't arrived yet, so there were only a few scattered pools of dirty brown water.

In the riverbed were people. Dozens and dozens of people. Women dipped circular metal pans in the dirty water. Men with shovels dug holes in the sand. Children sifted through the earth with their bare hands.

"What are they doing, Hery?"

"Looking for gemstones, Miss Hayley. Rubies, emeralds, sapphires. Just *one* discovery could change their lives."

"You mean they could buy a house with a swimming pool?"

"No, Miss Hayley. Maybe a generator to provide electricity or materials to build a small shop. Things like that would make a big difference."

"Do many people get lucky?" Dad asked.

"Very few, Mr Fletcher. But still, they keep trying."

I guess that people would do anything to help their families. To buy food. Or make their lives easier. It's all about money. We need it to survive.

The people in the riverbed look for shiny little rocks. Others catch and sell animals. Like Romeo and Juliet.

People collecting rocks is one thing, but people stealing living things is totally different. It's wrong! And now there was a plan to catch those terrible people. But would it work?

*   *   *

At breakfast the next morning, I found out the unwanted answer to that question.

"That's *dreadful*," Mum said. She drew our attention to the television screen, where there was a photo of the PHILIBERT'S REPTILE RESERVE sign. This was followed by video footage of the smouldering landscape of blackened trees. There clearly had been a forest fire.

The news headline read,

INCENDIE VOLONTAIRE!
AU RÉSERVE DES REPTILES

Mum translated for us, "'Arson at the Reptile Reserve' "

Someone had set fire to our reptile place. The one we visited. The one in the newspaper article.

Mum listened to the French carefully as a young woman behind the newsreaders desk finished this story before moving on to the weather.

"The animals!" Natalie said. "Were any of them..."

"I'm not sure, Nat," Mum said. "I only caught the end of the report."

"The animals are safe," Hery said, entering the hotel dining room. "I just spoke with my brother. He says the fire never reached the cages."

"That's a relief," Mum said.

"I bet our lemur-nappers did it," Hayley said. "I bet they read the newspaper article and went there to steal the chameleons. And when they realised they'd been tricked – that there were no newly-discovered chameleons – they got angry and started the fire."

"We don't know for sure, Hayley," Dad said. "It could have been an accident. You know, someone dropping a cigarette, something like that."

But I think that Dad, like the rest of us, was *pretty sure* who had started that fire. And my plan had failed. The criminals must've seen the police waiting for them. They avoided being captured and now knew that the police were watching for them to strike again. It would be very risky to commit another crime.

No crime, no arrest. No arrest, no confession. There was no hope of ever finding Romeo and Juliet.

Chapter 15

Surprise, Surprise!

not long ago there were more passenger pigeons in North America than any other bird. A single flock was so packed that it blocked out the sun for many miles. In the late 1800s and early 1900s, five billion of these creatures were hunted for food and sport. In 1914, Martha, the last of the passenger pigeons, died. Alone, in a concrete cage in a zoo.

We were nearing the end of yet *another* long drive. For most of that time, I managed to ignore voices in my head reminding me that my plan had failed. Mum's new word game was a welcome distraction.

"*Quack to the Future*!"

"Well done, Hayley," Dad said.

In Mum's new game you had to change the title of a book or film so it had something to do with *animals.*

"*A Tale of Two Kitties*," Mum said, then added, "Written by Charles Chickens."

My turn. "*Raiders of the Lost Shark*. Dad?"

"I say... "*Harry Otter and the Goblet of Fireflies*. Note the two animals in one! Over to you, Natalie."

"How about... *Foosabumps*?"

"Goosebumps," I explained to Hery. "Stories for kids. They're half-scary, half-funny."

"Fossabumps, Goosabumps," laughed Hery. "Good one, Miss Natalie."

He then became serious and told us all about fossas: how they hunted at dawn or dusk and were rarely seen by people."

"Aw, I was hoping to see one."

"It is not impossible, Miss Natalie. Last week, in this very park, tourists from New Zealand saw a mother fossa and her two pups."

"Maybe we'll be lucky, Nat," Mum said. "Whose turn is it?"

Hery took one hand off the steering wheel and raised his index finger, trying to get some attention.

main body is striped black and yellow. The legs and upper body are fire engine red and the wings are dark blue with white spots. It looks like it has been painted by an insane four-year-old!

And then on a small bush were the planthoppers. They are insects, but in the growing stage before they become adults. They look like small white flowers. When Mirana touched one it propelled itself into the air like a spring-loaded toy.

The island of Madagascar was full of surprises.

"Aaah... warm bottled water never tasted so good," Dad said.

"Especially with this – what it's called again, Hery?"

"Koba, Mrs Fletcher."

Hot and tired, we had stopped in a shaded clearing for a drink. Hery's mum had sent along some peanut-flavoured cake, a Malagasy speciality called koba.

"Yes, this is delicious," Natalie said.

"That's the least I can do, Miss Natalie. After failing to find your fossa."

"That's okay, Hery," Natalie said. "As always, I've seen a hundred other amazing things."

"Oh, I'm sorry, Hery," Mum said. "You haven't had a go."

"Thank you, Mrs Fletcher," he said, beaming like a six-year-old. "Do you all know the story of Snow White and the Seven Dwarf Lemurs?"

"I bet we're in for some surprises here," Dad said enthusiastically.

A short time later, wearing shorts and T-shirts, rucksacks on our backs, we were standing in another dusty, half-filled car park. The sign read MAINA FOREST.

"This place reminds me of the American southwest," Dad said. "Cowboy country."

"It seems very dry, doesn't it?" Mum observed.

"'Maina' means 'dry', Mrs Fletcher," Hery explained. "Most of the rain falls on the other side of the island. Our guide will tell us more...Ah, I think she is coming now." Hery pointed up ahead where a woman came striding towards us. Her name was Mirana and she was dressed in a green tracksuit and green trainers. Her lined face and short grey hair put her in an age category halfway between Dad and Nan... but she soon proved to be in better shape than any of us.

As we struggled to keep up with her fast-paced strides, she explained what Hery was telling us about Madagascar's rainfall, about the differences between this forest and the eastern ones we had visited earlier in the week.

"In the East, rain falls. Those forests are tropical jungles. In the West, no rain. Forests are semi-arid deserts."

You could see the differences. Here, there were many scraggy, dry-looking bushes and the few trees were spaced far apart. There was more blue sky above, but less shade from the hot sun.

Minutes into our walk, Mirana stepped off the trail. She examined a metre-high bush. It was leafless, revealing a skeleton of thin, grey branches. She silently motioned us over.

"What do you see?" Mirana whispered.

We stood for several moments staring at the bush.

"Wow, that's amazing!" Mum had seen something.

Then Hery and Hayley saw it. Then Natalie. Then me.

A stick insect. Remarkably camouflaged. Looking like just another branch.

"What?" Dad moaned. "I can't see anythi branches!"

My sisters and I kept pointing at the mo creature, trying to help.

"Dad, that's the head."

"And those skinny things are the legs."

"And those really skinny things are the ai

It didn't help. Dad only managed to se Mirana gently prodded it, sending it along the branch. We would be teasing I this for years!

"...And although once part of Africa, M has never had the large mammals: the the rhinos, the giraffes." Mirana was ar the island's smaller inhabitants. Especial ones. In addition to the stick insect, she other strange minibeasts. Like the gir This beetle looks like a cross between a M&M – and a construction site cra bright red body but otherwise is jet b jointed neck is three times the length its body. On its tiny head are two big and a pair of long bristled antennae.

Mirana also showed us the rainb locust, a massive multicoloured gra

"Make that about a hundred and twenty," Hayley said, pointing to the far side of the clearing. "Looks like we have company."

"*Maky*," whispered Mirana.

A group of ring-tailed lemurs! Walking right into the middle of our clearing.

We had seen other lemurs this trip, but these were the famous ones. The ones on the TV nature programmes. Seeing them in person and up close was pure magic.

Their fur was mostly grey, and they had white fox-like faces with intelligent-looking yellow eyes circled in black. And then, there were those tails – those long, black and white striped tails.

"This is their regular meeting place."

"What do you call a *group* of them, Mirana?" Mum asked. In France, we had talked about collective nouns: a *pack* of wolves or a *gaggle* of geese or a *murder* of crows. Or my all-time favourite – a *crash* of rhinos.

Mirana smiled. "They are a *conspiracy* of lemurs," she said.

Which made sense. A *conspiracy* was when a bunch of people (or the primate relatives of people!) make a secret plan to do something bad. Tails proudly pointing upwards, this conspiracy of lemurs strolled into the clearing like they owned the place, like they were scheming to take over the world.

Untroubled by our presence, some of them sat on their haunches nibbling leaves. Infant-carrying mothers socialised near a large boulder. One of the babies jumped down from his mother's back and ran towards us. Then, suddenly, he braked hard, made a high-pitched chirping sound and ran back to parental safety. Three adolescent lemurs fought over a piece of cake that Hery had thrown into the middle of the clearing.

As we watched these playful creatures, something in the distance caught my eye. Something in the bushes. Moving slowly through them. Two figures, one tall with a black hat and the other short with a white hat. Well, surprise, surprise! It was them. The lemur kidnappers!

Chapter 16

Time for Action

Fifty million years ago, a group of lemurs floated to Madagascar on a raft of vegetation. With the passing of the years, those first visitors evolved into the more than one hundred species that now inhabit the island. The most recognisable is the ring-tailed lemur, known for its long, black and white ringed tail. Because of the destruction of their forest homes and the illegal pet trade, just over 2,000 ring-tailed lemurs are alive today.

"I have to pee," I said, jumping up from the fallen log I had been sitting on.

"Can it wait, dear?" Mum asked. "There are toilets near the front gate."

"I'm sort of... desperate." I hopped around in a silly attempt to illustrate my desperation.

Mirana smiled, pointing towards some bushes. "Ladies to the left, gentlemen to the right."

"Be back soon, everybody." I hurried across the clearing, saying, "Excuse me, sir" to a fruit-nibbling lemur blocking my way, then disappeared into the bushes.

A few steps in, I could see the two brown-skinned figures moving slowly among the green vegetation. I could see that the short white-hatted one wore a large backpack and the tall, black-hatted one smoked a cigarette. I quietly followed them at a safe distance.

The two men stopped. I couldn't make out what they were saying – the words were indistinct and probably not in English – but they had made a decision of some sort. Changing direction, they started walking again, away from the clearing where my family waited for me.

I knew the sensible thing to do. I even started to do it. I began heading back to the clearing, where I would let the grown-ups take over and Mirana call the local police.

But then I thought about it. By the time the police arrived, the baddies would be long gone. So I decided to do the thing *opposite* to what was sensible when you are near two dangerous criminals: I kept following them. Pausing to look around, I found what I needed: a tree dwarfing the other bushes and trees. It was a baobab, that magnificent creature with a thick, smooth trunk crowned with root-like branches.

That tall baobab would be my landmark. If I kept it in sight, there was no way I could get lost. If I ran into any sort of trouble, I could turn around and find my way back. I tightened the straps on my backpack, and after taking a deep breath, I began walking, always keeping the tall black hat and short white hat in my sight.

There wasn't much vegetation to give me cover. Still, with quick spurts, I was able to pinball unseen from bush to bush or the occasional tree. The two men – I named them Tall Black and Short White – moved noiselessly. They spread out as if looking for something. Each of them would occasionally stop and bend over to examine the ground. Stopping. Moving. Stopping. Moving. What were they looking for?

I glanced back at my baobab. It had grown smaller, my view of it being restricted by the scattered trees closest to me. How much longer would I be able to count on it to find my way back to the others?

The silence of the forest was interrupted by a sharp whistle. Short White was excitedly waving to his companion, who ran up to join him. Together, they once again bent over and studied the ground. Moments later, they straightened up. Tall Black patted Short White's head in congratulatory fashion. They had found what they were looking for. They moved again, now with increased speed.

More time passed. The afternoon sun was low in the sky. Only the very tip of my baobab was visible.

Suddenly, Short White grabbed Tall Black by the shirt, urging him to stop. *Ssshhing* him with a raised forefinger, he pointed up ahead. I managed to quietly slip behind the trunk of a nearby tree.

The two men were standing in an open area of flat ground fringed with dense bushes and a few large boulders. In the clearing was an animal. Brown in colour, it was about the size of a large housecat, yet sleek and more powerful looking, similar to a North American mountain lion.

A fossa! It was probably a female because hiding behind it were two fossa pups. Miniature versions of their mother, they huddled together, partially screened off from the two men. Except for the occasional slow swish of her long, monkey-like tail, the mother fossa stood motionless. Muscles taut, teeth bared, she made no sound. She was ready to defend her babies.

Short White opened his backpack and removed a large dirty sack and slinked to the edge of the clearing. Tall Black picked up a branch from the ground and extended it towards the mother fossa, provoking her with repeated jabbing motions. The fossa responded with a drawn-out, guttural roar – followed by an unreal pounce into the air where she sunk her sharp teeth into the end of the branch. Tall Black yanked hard, dragging the fossa towards him.

The fossa's jaw relaxed, releasing her grip on the branch. She fell feet first to the ground, halfway between her tormentor and her offspring. Tall Black swung the branch madly about, disorientating the mother fossa and increasing the gap between her and her family.

As he began making chirping noises Short White slowly advanced towards the pups. Backed against a boulder, pressed together, the fossa siblings whimpered pathetically. But their mother was unable to help them. With the open sack in his hand, Short White cornered the vulnerable youngsters.

It was time for action.

Emerging from behind the tree, I charged into the clearing, yelling like a rampaging Viking warrior. Tall Black, surprised by the appearance of a berserk eleven-year-old, stopped swinging his branch for a single moment. That was all the time the mother fossa needed. She exploded across the clearing, past a startled Short White. In seconds, the mother fossa and her two little ones had disappeared into the undergrowth.

The fossas were safe.

But me? I was in trouble. Big trouble.

Chapter 17

Where are you Taking Me?

Although resembling members of the cat family, fossas are closely related to mongooses. As skilled hunters, they have been top predators in Madagascar for twenty million years. But now they are endangered. Their forests shrink yearly. Wild dogs – human pets gone astray – spread deadly germs. With the loss of habitat and life-threatening diseases, the fossas' population has become dangerously low.

I was trapped like a rat. Except a rat would dart away to safety. *Most* animals would be able to deal with my predicament. A gazelle would run like the wind. A squirrel would scamper up a tree. An armadillo would roll up into a protective ball. A badger would scratch and bite. Even a fragile butterfly would wing its way to freedom. But I was a human being, and a human being was quite helpless compared to most other members of the animal kingdom.

So I wasn't trapped like a rat. I was trapped like a small and weak and slow eleven-year-old boy.

My breathing was shallow and fast. I felt my heart thumping in my chest. I was afraid, very afraid.

The two men closed in on me. Short White still carried his dirty sack – would I fit inside? Tall Black was angry, his faced scrunched up, his mouth open.

And then Tall Black was directly in front of me, yelling at me. I didn't know what he was saying – the language was no doubt Malagasy – but I sure got the message! Along with his cigarette breath and bits of spit.

Short White touched his friend's elbow, speaking to him. Tall Black stopped yelling, though he continued to glare angrily, as Short White spoke to me. *Poo kwah fay tew sah?*

French maybe. Still, all I could do was look at him blankly. I managed to slow down my breathing, taking long deep breaths (like I learned once in a PE Yoga class taught by this supply teacher from California).

Short White tried again. "Why you do that?"

He spoke English! I breathed a quick sigh of relief. Knowing that Short White knew my language – even if it did have a bit of a French accent – made a difference. That somehow made the criminals seem less sinister. Not so evil. However, this reassurance was only temporary. Tall Black exploded again, ranting and raving as he aggressively pointed an index finger into my face.

Another touch from Short White again calmed him down.

"My friend – he is mad because – because you stop us."

Stopped you? I thought. It was my turn to be angry, and my anger pushed away my fear.

"Yes, I did stop you," I said, pointing at the dirty sack. "From stealing two baby fossas."

Tall Black tapped Short White on the shoulder, asking him something in his language. Short White must have translated what I had said because I

135

heard the word 'fossa'. Tall Blank said something back to his companion and laughed dismissively.

Short White pointed to Tall Black. "He say, 'We do not see fossa.'"

Yeah, sure *you didn't.*

Tall Black said something else.

"Yes," Short White said, again translating for me. "We do not see fossa. You do not see fossa. No fossa, so there is no problem."

"No fossas?" I said. But they were right. The fossas had escaped. No crime was committed. I should have stopped there. But I didn't. "Then what about the *lemurs*?"

"*What* lemurs?" Short White asked, glancing back slyly at Tall Black.

"The ones you stole from the Conservation..." I shut up, but too late.

"Lemurs..." Short White said. "Yes, the lemurs. You know about them? *Now* there is a problem."

This was not good. The two men knew that *I* knew they were the ones who kidnapped Romeo and Juliet.

"Please do not run." Short White said, turning to speak with Tall Black. He pointed to his friend, adding, "He has long legs. He is very fast."

The criminals began talking together – no doubt discussing what to do with me.

As they talked, I finally got a really good look at them.

They weren't men at all. They were boys. Teenagers really. Younger than Hery. Still, they were criminals – capable of stealing innocent animals and who knows what else...

I tried to break in. "You know, my family – my family knows where I am. They are coming to find me."

Short White interrupted his conversation only long enough to have a quick look around at the scrubby desert landscape. Not another soul could be seen. Without responding to me, he continued his conversation.

When he had finished, he turned to me.

"Come."

"Where are you taking me? I don't really—"

"*Avy*!" said Tall Black, waving me to start moving. He didn't yell, but the tone of his words was dripping with menace.

Earlier in the afternoon, I should have waited for grown-ups. A few moments ago I should have kept my mouth shut. Two mistakes. And now I found myself walking, like a prisoner between two cold-hearted guards. Away from the Baobab tree landmark. Away from the people I loved.

Through the dry landscape, the three of us walked, a fast pace, without breaks to rest, without conversation. Unpleasant thoughts rattled around in my head: places they were taking me, things they might do to me.

By now the sun was just above the horizon, and I felt a slight chill in the air. The high temperature of a Madagascar day drops very quickly!

We had been walking on unmarked ground through a landscape that all looked the same to me. Tall Black and Short White walked with purpose. Were they regular visitors to this forest? Or maybe they just knew how to navigate their way through nature, like America's Native Americans or the people living in the Amazon rainforest.

All of a sudden, at a place where a dirt trail crossed our unmarked route, the two young men stopped. Tall Black lit up another cigarette. Short White produced two small bottles of water from his backpack. He handed one to his smoking friend.

"Where – where are you taking me?" I said quietly.

"Okay…" I tried to remember some of the other words or phrases that Hery had taught us. One popped into my head. Waving my hand, I said, "Salama. *Manao ahoana ianao*!"

They laughed – no doubt at my rubbish pronunciation. Short White repeated the greeting to me and held out his hand. Tall Black gave me a half-hearted nod of his head. (I think that he still did not like me very much.)

"*Iza ny anaranao*?" Short White asked.

I *knew* that one! He had asked me my name. "*Brandon no anarako*."

Short White pointed to himself. "*Olana no anarako*." He smiled again – a friendly, playful smile. "In my language, *Olana* means 'trouble'. My mother and father, they pick right name for me!"

I pointed to Tall Black. "*Iza ny anaranao*?"

Tall Black rolled his eyes dismissively. "*Lova no anarako*," he mumbled.

"Lova means 'rich'," Olana said, laughing. "*His* mother pick wrong name! Lova is 'rich' but Lova is *not* rich!"

Olana and Lova. Now that I knew their names, I could think of them as real people, not horrible baddies. They still *might* be horrible, but they were also two teenagers named Olana and Lova.

Olana asked me to say something else.

I knew how to count to three, so I pointed to each of us in turn. "*Iray... roa... telo*." And I showed off my favourite phrase in Malagasy: "*Tsy manambady aho*."

Olana again laughed. "I too. I am not married. Never!" He jerked a thumb in Lova's direction. "But this – this big *mamono*—"

"*Mamono*?"

"I don't know in English." Olana stood up tall and aggressively beat his chest in an ape-like fashion.

"A gorilla?"

"No. Not gorilla. With orange hair."

"Oh, you mean an orangutan!"

"Yes, this big orangutan – *he* wants to marry. To daughter of butcher. But there is problem."

"What is it?" I asked.

"No money. For *moletry*."

"*Moletry*?" I asked.

"*Fanomezana*. Gifts. From family of boy to father of girl."

"What sort of gifts?"

Olana rubbed his left thumb against the index finger and middle finger of the same hand. This gesture I recognised as 'very expensive' gifts.

"American refrigerator or Italian motor scooter." He grinned. "Before was easy: you steal zebu, you give zebu to father of girl. You marry girl."

Lova seemed to understand. Lighting up another cigarette, he said something to Olana and the two of them laughed.

"Yes," said Olana. "In Madagascar zebu are everywhere. But *money*?" He pretended to scan the landscape around him, looking for something – but not locating it. "Money is... is *zara raha*. I don't know how to say in English."

"*Hard to find*?" I suggested.

"Yes, hard to find. Not enough money. For food. For clothing. Maybe small generator to make electricity."

There was a long awkward silence. I looked up at the sky. The sun was just above the horizon. The day was nearly over. "Er – Olana. Lova. My parents – my mother and father – they are worried. Do you think I can – you know, I would like to—"

"You would like to go."

I nodded.

Olana said something to Lova, who (as he lit up yet another cigarette) said something back. "One moment, please," Olana said. He and Lova began talking in low voices. I stood there quietly. Thinking.

These people – they were criminals. But they didn't seem like *bad people*. They *did* kidnap innocent animals. But they desperately needed *money*. Everybody needs money, right? Was it okay to do bad things so your family could eat and have decent clothes? Or to buy something that might make their difficult lives more bearable?

Confusion was still swirling around my head when Olana and Lova finished their discussion. "Come," Olana said. "We will help you." We turned right on the dirt trail and started walking again.

As we continued through the dry forest, Lova puffed away at cigarettes and Olana asked me question after question. About London. About myself. I soon felt relaxed enough to ask them a little bit about *their* lives. I found out that they lived in a completely different world than me. Their parents couldn't find decent jobs. They never went to a doctor. Most of their clothes were bought second-hand in the local market.

But the conversation wasn't *always* depressing. With Olana doing loads of translating for me and Lova, we talked about football and video games and families. That last topic even brought a proper smile to Lova's face: he, too, was tormented by two irritating sisters! I think that he had finally decided that I was all right.

The sunlit clarity of day was long gone when we stopped for the last time together. Here, another trail crossed the one on which we were standing. Olana and Lova had one of their hushed conversations, this discussion less heated than the last one. Still, I sensed some disagreement between the two friends.

Olana finally emerged from the conversation. "It is good idea... for you to wait."

"That's okay. I understand." Somebody might be looking for me and see them. They needed a bit of a head start. "How long?" I looked up at the darkening sky. "Will ten minutes be enough?"

"Please. Fifteen is better."

"Sure. I'll wait fifteen minutes. But which way do I go?"

"That is easy," said Olana. He picked up a short sharp stick and pointed left along the trail. "That way." Then, in the dirt, he drew a line representing the trail, with intersecting lines indicating where other trails crossed. "One, two, three..." Olana said, counting off the crossed trails. "At the third trail turn left. Walk more. You will see four very big rocks."

"Boulders?"

"I think yes. At boulders turn right. Walk five minutes. You will find gate. People to help you."

"Thank you, Olana" I said, then added. "Thank you, too, Lova."

"Now we must go," Olana said.

Olana held out his hand and I shook it. Lova, after flicking the end of his cigarette away, also shook my hand. The two teenagers began walking away. Looking back over his shoulder, Olana waved to me, shouting, "*Veloma*!"

"*Veloma*!" I shouted back, returning his wave. In the gathering dusk, the two teenagers moved through the forest. The last I saw of them was Lova's hat bobbing above the bushes, like a tiny black boat sailing across a shadowy green sea.

Slumping against a tree trunk, I breathed a massive sigh of relief. What a crazy afternoon! It started with fiends – and ended with friends!

Yes, the day looked like it would end with a happy ending.

In a short time I would be reunited with my family.

Chapter 19

alone in the Forest

natives of Southeast Asia, orangutans have lived on Earth for over fourteen million years. But now, much of their forest habitat is being destroyed by fires or cut down for farming. Every year orangutan mothers are killed to capture their babies for the illegal international pet trade. These clever and shy primates – relatives of humans and the other great apes – are close to extinction.

I had no watch or phone to know when fifteen minutes were up. So I used a trick learned from an Australian supply teacher, something to mark off a minute: count to 60, with saying each number followed by the word 'kangaroo'. Do that fifteen times, that would be fifteen minutes. Then I could start off.

"One kangaroo, two kangaroo, three kangaroo, four kangaroo, five kangaroo, six..."

A few seconds into the first minute my counting came to a stop. I had smelled something. Smoke. Nearby, rising from a tuft of grass, was a thin wisp of white vapour. It must have come from Lova's discarded cigarette. (Maybe the fire at the reptile place *had been* just a careless accident.)

The grass burst into flame. Jumping up and down vigorously, I quickly smothered the tiny blaze. The tuft of grass re-ignited.

Dealing with the problem wasn't going to be that easy. Time for a different strategy. I unzipped my shorts, and while loudly humming a sloppy version of the theme from *Star Wars*, I peed on the new flame. Hissing in defeat, the fire went out. Mission accomplished.

After tossing a few handfuls of dirt on the dark patch of damp ground, I stayed a bit longer to make sure there were no more hot spots. I finished counting off the minutes.

The directions to the park gate seemed quite straightforward: at the fourth intersecting trail, turn left and continue, then turn right at the three boulders – and from there it was a short walk to someone who could help me return to my family.

The sun was long gone and there was still no sign of the three boulders. More worryingly, the trail had disappeared. Had I made a mistake? I pushed from my mind the possibility that Olana and Lova had given me false directions.

Stopping to rest, I took off my rucksack. I drank the last of my water. As I finished off the remaining six raspberry bonbons, I looked around me. With the setting of the sun, the bushes and trees had darkened, drained of daytime colour. The sky had become a dark shade of blue. The air felt cooler. The night – and despair – were quickly closing in on me.

Then, in the distance, I saw something that gave me hope. Root-like branches rising above the other trees. My landmark! My arms extended in an invitation for a virtual hug, I whooped loudly. "I love you, baobab!"

My gaze drifted to the right. What? Another distant baobab. Turning a slow 360 degrees, I counted one... two... three... four more baobabs. "I hate you, baobabs!" I shouted, uselessly shaking my fist.

The baobabs all looked the same. I had to stay put. To stay in one place and hope that help would arrive.

But after a short time, no help had arrived. Except for a massive black butterfly with white spots, I hadn't seen another living thing. The Madagascan sky had quickly gone from blue to dark blue to very dark blue... and now to black. Far from the light of any city, out in the middle of nowhere, this was a proper darkness. I felt the fear that my cave-dwelling ancestors must have felt.

I looked skywards. Millions of stars. The stars in India had been magical. These stars were without magic. Remote and lifeless, producing neither warmth nor hope.

I started at the sound of some rustling in the nearby bushes. *Relax, Brandon.* Probably some lizard. (I wasn't worried about wild animals. Hery said that fossas never attack humans and most of the snakes in Madagascar were on the other side of the island.)

No, animals were not the problem. Neither was thirst or hunger. (Dad once told me that people can go three days without water and even longer without food.)

The problem was the cold. Dressed only in shorts and a T-shirt I sat there shivering violently while my teeth chattered like one of those stupid wind-up toys.

I was filled with despair. I didn't know how I could survive until the morning.

Then I saw something. In the blackness, high in the trees were two tiny pinpoints of red light. The eyes of an aye-aye!

I thought about another pair of red eyes, the one belonging to that old man. I wondered again why he had chosen *me*, why he had given me the strange postcard and the horn.

The *horn*. I had forgotten about the horn!

My rucksack was on the ground beside me. With numb fingers, I managed to open the zip. Groping around inside I quickly located the polished smooth bone, removed it from my pack and brought it to my lips. I took a deep breath... and blew as hard as possible.

The result was the same as before: nothing.

Then I remembered something Hery had said. That in order to make a sound, you had to *be the horn*. Still shivering, I again brought the horn to my lips. Trying to ignore the bitter cold, I started taking slow, deep breaths. *Be the horn*... I am the horn... I am the boy-horn... I am Horn Boy.

I inhaled again, pulling the chilly air deep into my lungs. Then I breathed out a slow, sustained flow of air – out of my lungs through my mouth and into the horn. The horn and I were one and the same.

And then it happened. A noise. Not the proud, defiant blast of a Merina warrior. (More like the stifled squawk of his little pet dog getting its tail stepped on.) But it was a beginning.

Be the horn. I blew again. The sound was a bit louder. Once more. *Be the horn.* I blew and there was a strong trumpeting sound, loud and long and clear, a call resounding throughout the forest: "*I AM HERE!*"

I blew again and again and again. Finally, too exhausted to blow any more, I slumped to the ground, my back against a tree. I wrapped my arms tightly around my shivering body and closed my eyes.

Chapter 20
Safe and Sound

Titanoboa was the largest snake that ever lived. It prowled the swamps of South America around fifty million years ago. At 13 metres long, it was twice the length of today's giant anaconda. The reasons for its extinction are unknown, though it probably died out during one of Earth's catastrophic ice ages.

After a short and broken sleep, I was awakened by a sound. It wasn't the sound of something alive, like a hoot or a grunt or a growl. It was a mechanical noise. A horn. Not the long, sustained sound of my zebu blowing horn; this sound was an irregular pattern of short, sharp bursts. Like from a car!

The honking stopped. Rubbing my eyes, I sat up, stiff with cold. Millions of stars still packed the black sky. Darkness. Yet there was something else. In the distance, in the darkness. A flickering light. Yes, the trees and bushes were flickering with white light. Something was moving through the forest, some sort of vehicle.

Now more alert, I fumbled for the zebu horn lying on the ground beside me. I managed to struggle to my feet and I once again became the horn. I loved that deep rich sound!

The lights in the forest seemed to change direction. They were now coming directly towards me, two blazing circles of brightness. A vehicle! My signal for help had worked!

Moments later, I was blinded by the headlights of a small pick-up truck as it entered the clearing. The truck came to a complete stop – and out jumped Dad! He ran over and wrapped his arms around me, hugging me like a deranged gorilla.

"Mr Brandon, you would make a fine Merina warrior." It was Hery! Out of the corner of my teary eyes I saw him, bending over to pick up my horn and rucksack. Dad wrapped me in a fleecy jacket and bundled me into the truck.

Mirana was behind the wheel. Dad squeezed in beside me; Hery climbed into the open back of the truck. Mirana smiled at me, handing me a bottle of water and a small pack of chocolate biscuits. She started the engine and turned on the heat, an enveloping rush of life-restoring warmth.

Water, food, heat. I felt alive again. "What time is it?" I asked.

"Twelve hours later than the last time I saw you," Dad said. "About two in the morning."

"Where's Mum? And Natalie and Hayley?"

"They're fine, Bran. You'll see them soon. For now just rest."

"Okay, Dad." He was right. My alertness had not lasted long. Now I felt drained, both emotionally and physically. I gazed sleepily out the truck window. The world was a waking dream. Winding in and out in the dark forest... speeding along a proper road... driving on a dirt road past a BAOBAB RESORT sign. And then rolling to a complete stop.

I remember Mum waiting in the darkness. Another bone-crushing hug. Dad carrying me into some small building. Getting tucked into a nice comfortable bed. Two kisses on my forehead and

Mum and Dad saying, 'Good night, Brandon.' I don't remember if I managed a "Good Night" in return before falling asleep.

I awoke to the loud chirping of a nearby bird. Wonderfully refreshed, I sat up, basking in the warm sunlight coming through the thin curtains of the room. Nearby, in two other single beds, my sisters soundlessly slept.

I threw off the light blanket that covered me and slid out of bed. Quickly throwing on my shorts and T-shirt, I grabbed my trainers off the wooden floor and tiptoed towards the door.

The door opened onto a wooden porch with a wooden bench. The building where I had slept was a hut that had an A-shaped, thatch-covered roof. Sitting down on the bench, I put on my shoes and bounced down three steps onto a gravel path.

I was thirsty. I was hungry. But I was alive – and it was time to explore the Baobab Resort.

The gravel path meandered through the resort's natural setting. Among the bushes and trees – including a few baobabs – were other huts, all of the same design. (Mum and Dad's was probably the one across the path from where my sisters and I had slept.) It was peaceful. The only sounds were the incessant twitterings of that crazy bird and the nearby swishing of a woman sweeping leaves from the path with a broom made from branches.

I followed the path past the last hut. There, where the bushes and trees disappeared, was a larger wooden building. My rumbling stomach, our "second brain" according to Dad, informed me that this was the resort's restaurant. On the patio surrounding the circular building was a man setting out chairs around tables. He looked at me and waved. I waved back before continuing my exploration.

I next discovered the swimming pool. Large and rectangular, its wooden deck was furnished with lounge chairs and umbrellas. With the day quickly heating up, the pool's clear blue water looked very tempting.

At the poolside bar – now closed – I climbed up onto a high stool and thought about yesterday. About Olana and Lova again. People trying to survive in a tough world. Couldn't they manage without stealing innocent creatures? Maybe they had no choice...

Thoughts about desperate people and lost lemurs were interrupted by more grumbling of my stomach. It was time to get the others up for breakfast. I slid down off the barstool and made my way back to the huts.

"Did they have knives? Or guns? Or maybe some—"

"Hayley!" Over breakfast, Mum was still distressed about my disappearance. She turned to me. "Brandon, you had us so worried. Those men – they could have—"

"I know, Mum. I'm sorry. I shouldn't have gone after them alone. But really – it turned out they weren't that bad."

"Not that bad?" challenged Hayley. "They're heartless animal kidnappers!"

"I know, but..." I couldn't sort out in my *own* mind how bad Olana and Lova really were; it was even more difficult trying to explain that to others.

So I kept to the simple facts, recounting (between bites of a massive omelette!) what had happened yesterday. I must admit I played up the bit about saving the fossas.

"I still can't believe you got to see a mother and two babies," Natalie said.

"And thanks to Bran's quick thinking and bravery," Dad said, "those fossa pups are back safely with their mother."

"Yes," Mum said, her eyes glistening with emotion. "A mother and her children need to be together."

Hayley spoke. "The important thing is that Brandon knows what the kidnappers look like. He can tell a police artist and their faces will be pasted all over Madagascar."

"You think you could describe them, son?" Dad asked.

"Of course, I could... I mean, I'm not sure..."

"Not sure?" Hayley said. "You were with them for *hours*."

"I know, but... but I didn't really get a good look at them. For one thing, they were wearing hats. Plus, the sun was in my eyes. And I was a bit frightened so didn't—"

"You must remember something," Hayley insisted. "Were they fat or skinny? Tall or short? What were they *wearing*?"

I snapped my fingers. "Yes, I remember what they were wearing!"

The others waited expectantly for me to tell them.

"They were wearing... clothes!"

Hayley rolled her eyes. Natalie burst into giggles. *"They were wearing clothes!* I mean, they wouldn't be naked, would they?"

Dad, Hayley and I laughed. Even Mum managed a smile.

Chapter 21

The Final Clue

Gorillas have been living in Africa for over seven million years. Highly intelligent, they make and use tools, produce sounds to communicate and care for sick and elderly members in their troop. They even laugh. But gorilla numbers are dropping fast. Humans hunt these shy creatures – our primate relatives – and cut down their forests.

We stayed at The Baobab Resort for two more days. Mum spent time with the restaurant cook and learned some local recipes. Hery introduced Dad to a traditional Malagasy board game where you tried to capture your opponent's counters. Dad – whether he had white counters or black ones – lost every single time. Hayley finally got around to her geography homework, sneakily backdating entries for her daily journal. Natalie taught Zecko the Gecko how to draw, but why the stuffed reptile's picture of a baobab tree was better than hers was beyond *my* comprehension. ('*I pr-pr-pr-practice m-m-more than N-N-Natalie,*' he said.)

Me? I made friends with the eleven-year-old son of a woman who worked at the resort (the same woman I had seen sweeping the path). Stenny didn't speak any English – I don't think he even went to school – but we still managed to communicate and have fun. Each day, after he finished his chores, we went cycling on dirt trails around the resort and played pétanque.

All of us spent many hours in or around the pool, swimming and sipping cold drinks.

On the morning of the third day, we packed up and started the long drive back to Tana. By early evening we walked through the doors of The Three Musketeers hotel for what I thought would be our last night in Madagascar.

THE FINAL CLUE

Later, in bed, I was in for a little surprise. When I turned over my pillow – I like sleeping on the cool side – I discovered that missing postcard. Finding it made me again start thinking about Madagascar's wildlife. When we got back home, I would make a display of the cards and photos Dad took of these remarkable animals: the birds, the chameleons and geckos, the minibeasts. And of course – the lemurs.

This postcard would be in the middle of the display. Romeo and Juliet would live forever, the centrepiece of a bulletin board in London, England.

The drive *back* to the airport was as quiet as the one we had made in the opposite direction ten days ago. Then it was because of exhaustion – from our long trip from London. I was definitely worn out: from Madagascar's draining mixture of wonder and excitement and misfortune. But this was different. The silence seemed to be one of sadness.

From the back seat, I caught sight of Hery smiling at me in the rear-view mirror. I was going to miss him; Madagascar, as I've said before (and will probably say for the rest of my life) is an amazing place, filled with plants and animals beyond compare. But I'm beginning to realise that it's the memories of *people* that make you feel all happy and sad inside. In Turkey, it was Javed. In India, there was JB and the Varma family. And in France, it was my friend Luke. Here it was Hery. Our guide and driver. Our friend.

At airport departures, luggage was unloaded onto the pavement. It was now time to say our goodbyes.

"Thanks, Hery – for everything," Dad said, slipping an envelope with money into Hery's shirt pocket.

"Thank you, Mr Fletcher," Hery said, handing back the envelope. "But I really can't – I mean, you are my friends and—"

"Please take it," Dad insisted, returning it to Hery's pocket.

"Think, Hery," I teased. "You might need it to buy a motor scooter for Tatiana's father." Everybody in my family gave me a puzzled look. "I'll explain it to you guys later."

Hery got back in the minivan and rolled down the window. "I will miss the Fletchers," he said. "Mrs Fletcher's word games. Mr Fletcher's lists of ice creams and top-selling cars in the UK. Miss Hayley's jokes. Mr Brandon's bravery..."

"What about me?" asked Natalie.

"Oh, yes. How could I forget Miss Natalie? I will miss your questions."

"Huh? Do I ask a lot of questions?"

"You're doing it again!" said Hayley.

"Am I?"

We all laughed. Hery started the minivan and pulled away from the kerb. We kept waving until he disappeared down the road.

Picking up our luggage, we walked into the airport terminal.

"Brandon, are you forgetting something?" Dad said. He pointed through the glass door. Outside, on the pavement, was my rucksack.

"Oops. Just be a sec." Leaving my small suitcase with the others, I ran outside and picked up the rucksack. I turned to re-enter the terminal building – and there he was: the man with red eyes, the white beard and the brown straw hat.

He was walking towards me. As he passed, he pushed another parcel into my hands. Plain brown paper, tied up with string. And then he was gone. I put the parcel in my rucksack and rejoined my family. Right now we were on the move. I badly wanted to open the parcel, but would have to wait.

We spent an hour and a half queueing up for check-in, queueing up for security, queueing up to board the plane. Now it was nearly take-off time. I sat in window Seat 17a, aching with curiosity. What was inside the parcel?

"Open it, Brandon," pleaded Natalie, who was sitting in the middle seat. Hayley looked on from the aisle seat. Mum and Dad stood behind us, waiting expectantly.

I broke the string and tore off the brown paper. I held up the parcel's contents for all to see.

"A T-shirt?" said Natalie.

It was a T-shirt with a cartoon lemur on it. The cartoon lemur held up another T-shirt. The lemur looked like a souvenir seller in the local market.

"It's another Romeo – or Juliet."

Mum was right. The lemur on the T-shirt had small, green eyes, and a brown head with a white star. How did the T-shirt makers know about them?

"I like the recursion," said Dad, looking over my shoulder.

"What is *that*?" asked Natalie.

"It's like a pattern, Nat. One that goes on forever."

I looked carefully at the T-shirt. Oh, yeah, I could see what Dad was talking about. On the T-shirt held up by the lemur was the same lemur – smaller, of course – selling another T-shirt. On *that* shirt, you could just make out an even smaller lemur selling a T-shirt.

"That's *wild*," said Hayley. "So, even though we can't see it, we know that each T-shirt shows a lemur selling a T-shirt with a lemur selling a T-shirt with a lemur selling a T-shirt... forever and ever.

"Yep," Dad said. "That's recursion."

Interesting, but more importantly, why a picture of the kidnapped lemur. Why did the man with the red eyes give it to me?

There was a crackling sound, signalling an aeroplane announcement. *"This is Captain Yıldız speaking. Cabin Crew ready for take-off."*

Mum and Dad sat back down in their seats and buckled up.

"Captain Yıldız," Natalie said. "That's the pilot from before. The one who teased Brandon about not knowing about soap."

"Well remembered, Natalie," I said. Every Saturday, crates of soap came to Madagascar, and every Wednesday – that was today – out went the crates filled with...

My head involuntarily swivelled towards the plane's small window, my eyes taking in the familiar runway tarmac scene. A fuel tanker here, a baggage transporter there. And the crates. Wednesday's crates. The ones filled with T-shirts.

T-shirts.

I looked at my new lemur T-shirt, then again looked out the window. That was when I noticed something. Something different. Is that what the man with the red eyes was trying to tell me?

I unfastened my seat belt and climbed over my sisters. "Wait! Stop the plane!"

Chapter 22

A Strange Scratching Sound

Homo sapiens have lived on Earth for 300,000 years. They have built cities and computers. They have travelled to outer space and inside the human cell. They create music, art and literature. Yet humans are also capable of destruction. They cut down forests; pollute the seas; raise the planet's temperature to dangerous levels; create situations that increase the chance of having deadly pandemics. If human beings do not change their behaviour, their actions will lead to the extinction of many living things. Including themselves.

I felt the stares of baffled passengers as a flight attendant in a red skirt and red blouse walked down the aisle towards me.

"Excuse me, can I help you?" Her words were courteous, but the tone of her voice leaked annoyance.

"I need to speak to Captain Yıldız... it's an emergency."

"The captain cannot—"

"I'll handle this, Zeyneb." It was Captain Yıldız. Pilot cap in his hand, he politely waved the flight attendant away. Then he looked at me. "I know *you*."

"From before, Captain Yıldız. About ten days ago. My name's Brandon Fletcher. And I have something really important to tell you."

"Let's go where we can talk." He led me to the cabin crew area at the back of the plane and pulled the curtain. "So, Brandon Fletcher, what's on your mind?"

"Well, I don't know if you remember, but ten days ago, when we landed in Mauritius, you told us about those crates. The big ones on the runway."

"I do remember. Soap comes in, T-shirts go out."

"Yes, exactly." I took a deep breath. "Well, there's something wrong."

"Wrong?"

"Yes. You see, when we arrived here, I counted the crates."

"Twenty-six," Captain Yıldız said. "Every week it's the same number."

"*Ten days ago* there were twenty-six. But when I counted today..."

The captain looked out the small window. After several moments he turned back to me. "That's odd... "

"Twenty-seven. Right?"

"Yes... but why?" the captain said, mostly to himself. "Why is there an extra crate?"

"I think *I* know why." I quickly told Captain Yıldız the story of the kidnapped lemurs. How the criminals needed to somehow get them out of the country. "I guess I just put two and two together..."

"And came up with twenty-seven!" Captain Yıldız smiled. He put his cap on and pulled back the curtain. "Come, Brandon Fletcher. Let's go have a look!"

Fifteen minutes later Captain Yıldız, my family and I were standing on the runway tarmac. The captain was pointing at the stacked crates, speaking with a man wearing a suit. The man in the suit made a call on his mobile phone, and almost immediately half a dozen men and women in yellow high-vis jackets arrived on the scene. One of them carried a black crowbar.

As the six airport employees unstacked the crates, I glanced over my shoulder, up towards the parked plane, where faces filled every window.

With the crates now laid out, we stood watching as the man with the crowbar went to work on one. Nails squealed as he slowly removed one of the rectangular slats that made up the crate's wooden lid. A woman reached through the opening and pulled out something: a T-shirt. A T-shirt with a picture of a baobab tree.

The man with the crowbar moved to the adjacent crate.

Another T-shirt, this one with a colourful chameleon. Crate after crate produced T-shirt after T-shirt, like rabbits being pulled from a magician's hat. T-shirts with ring-tailed lemurs, humpbacked whales, purple orchids, vanilla beans, swimming green turtles, Madagascar flags, fossas... In a short time, most of the crates lay open on the runway. With each new T-shirt, my initial high point of excitement dropped lower and lower. Maybe I had been wrong. Maybe the T-shirt given to me by the man with the red eyes wasn't a clue for *anything*.

"Sorry, Brandon," Dad said.

"It's okay, Dad," I said. "I guess I made a mistake. I wanted so badly to..."

"What, Brandon? Is something wrong?" Dad must've noticed that my attention had slipped away.

"Dad, did you just hear something?"

"No... I don't think so..."

"There it is again." A sound. A muffled scratching noise. This time, Dad heard the sound.

"I think... it came from inside *that* one," Dad said, indicating the unopened crate to our left.

"Quickly! Over here!" I shouted.

In seconds, the man with the crowbar was back at work. Getting Captain Yıldız's attention, I pointed at myself, then at the crate: my eyes silently saying, *Can I move closer?* The captain nodded his head, granting my voiceless request. I edged closer to the source of those scratching sounds.

One slat had already been removed from the top of the crate. And a second one. Bending over, I peered into the crate's shadowy interior. Only darkness. But wait, no. There was something else. Movement.

"In here!" I yelled.

The man in the suit barked out instructions and the five other airport workers surrounded the crate. My family and Captain Yıldız joined me. The man with the crowbar removed a third slat, then backed away.

We waited. And waited some more. Then, ever-so-slowly, a head rose from the hole in the crate. With small rounded ears and green eyes, it was brown except for a white, star-shaped patch on its forehead. And then a second head, nearly identical, emerged next to the first one. Our missing lemurs!

Romeo and Juliet blinked in the sunlight, anxiously flicking their heads this way and that. How long had they been confined to this small space? Unable to move. With no food. Disorientated and weak from hunger, they now made no effort to run away.

Then things happened fast. A phone call from the man in the suit. The arrival of a small white pick-up truck. The unloading of a matching pair of metal cages.

From her pocket, the driver of the pickup removed a small plastic bag with mango pieces. Using the irresistible fruit as bait, she coaxed

Romeo and Juliet out of the crate and into the cages.

We all waved goodbye as the truck drove the two lemurs away.

Captain Yıldız saluted me in congratulations. Natalie, who was now standing at my side, repeatedly tapped me on the arm. "Brandon, you're a hero!"

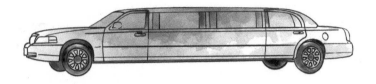

Chapter 23

a Five-Star Reception

Lemurs, inhabitants of Madagascar for fifty million years, are in serious trouble. Of the 104 known species, 75 are classified as either Endangered or Critically Endangered. Every day more forest is cut down, leaving them without homes, food and protection. These unique creatures, our evolutionary ancestors, are getting closer and closer to extinction.

I suppose that Natalie was right! I *was* sort of a hero. After our bags were taken off the plane, we were chauffeured back to Tana in a black limousine taxi. There, Hayley's life-long dream came true when we were treated to a one-night stay in a five-star hotel. (Tomorrow we would fly home.)

First, a report had to be made so that afternoon we went to the police station. A female officer dressed in a dark blue uniform asked me questions. I answered most of them truthfully, leaving out the details normal people would have trouble believing. Like the bit about an old man with red eyes who kept showing up with unusual gifts.

A gift of postcards that got me involved in a mystery. A gift of a blowing horn that probably saved my life. And a gift of a T-shirt which led to the rescue of the kidnapped lemurs. Like the red-eyed aye-aye, the red-eyed man seemed to be watching over the safety of Madagascar's lemurs.

"The two missing lemurs," the police officer said. "How did you know the lemurs were in one of those crates?"

"Um... er... those two guys. Yeah, in the forest. I overheard them say 'airport'." (Lucky for me, the word for 'airport' in Malagasy is – *airport*!)

"And can you describe these men?" the police officer said.

Suppressing a smile, I fought back the urge to say, *"They were wearing clothes."* What was funny with my family would be very stupid with a police officer. Instead, I told her that the two men were quite young. And that one of them was tall, and the other was short.

I knew the description wasn't enough to help the police catch anyone. I guess that was what I wanted. For Olana and Lova to have another chance. To prove that they weren't really bad people.

That night we were guests of honour at some famous restaurant. We shared a table with the mayor of Antananarivo and other important people. Even Hery was there! (Dad had secretly arranged for him to get invited.)

After dessert, the mayor stood up to make a speech. He was a chubby man dressed in a black suit with a green tie. He first told some joke about a lemur and a chameleon going into a bar. My sisters and I didn't get the punchline, but the grown-ups laughed like it was the funniest thing they'd ever heard.

The mayor then became serious and spoke about Madagascar's wildlife. How it was the country's number one treasure, and it needed to be protected. For now and for future generations. He also gave some ideas about how people could help. There were many wildlife conservation charities. Like the World Wildlife Fund or America's Lemur Conservation Foundation. They all needed money: to stop the illegal pet trade, and generally to educate people about the importance of our planet's plants and animals.

At the end of his speech, the mayor asked me to stand beside him and he thanked me for helping to rescue the two new lemurs. He said that he hoped my family and I would return to Madagascar, that it was a large island and there was so much more to see.

"And on behalf of all Malagasy people, I would like to present you with a small token of our appreciation."

I glanced at Hery at the end of the table, who was giving me the thumbs up and a big smile.

Then the mayor gave me a tiny chameleon in a cage for me to take back to England as a pet.

JUST JOKING! He *really* gave me a medal that said 'Madagascar' on it with a picture of a ring-tailed lemur. He shook my hand and all the people in the banquet room clapped for me. It was embarrassing. (But it also felt great!)

Early the next morning, Hery drove us to the newspaper office where his brother worked. In the minivan, we talked about how each of us could help the planet.

"I think we should take out a family membership for the World Wildlife Fund," Dad said.

"I'm going to buy all my Christmas and birthday gifts from their catalogue," Mum added.

Hayley said she would never buy earrings made out of ivory and Natalie was going to subscribe to a charity wildlife magazine.

"How about you, Brandon?" Natalie asked.

"Me? I think I'll adopt an endangered animal." You can give money to a charity to help protect an endangered species. The charity would send you a photo of a real animal and an adoption certificate. It was like having a pet in some exotic place.

"Which animal do you plan on adopting, Bran?" Dad asked. "Giant Panda? Rhino? Dolphin?"

"I – I don't know. I hadn't really thought about it. Maybe a snow leopard. Or a mountain gorilla. Or—"

"How 'bout a Hery?"

Huh? My younger sister had finally gone completely bonkers!

"What do you mean, dear?" Mum asked. "Hery doesn't *need* adopting. He has a very nice mother."

"But he's *critically endangered.*"

"Because...?" Hayley challenged, her arms folded across her chest.

"Because there's only one of him left in the world!"

We were still laughing when Hery parked in front of the newspaper office.

Hery's brother, Andy Rakoto, was shorter than Hery, thinner but with the same friendly smile. While the rest of my family and Hery had a tour of the newspaper office, Andy escorted me to a small room and interviewed me for a feature story. It was entitled "London Lad Liberates Lemurs". He asked me how I had solved the mystery of the missing lemurs plus all sorts of personal questions – about my hobbies, favourite book and film, what I want to be when I grow up, things like that.

And if I had a girlfriend. *No!* Why do people always ask me that?!

"One last question, Brandon," Andy said. "What do you like best about Madagascar?"

That was easy. "The lemurs!"

When the interview ended, it was time for photos. First me by myself. Then one of the whole family.

"You too, Hery," Dad said. "Get in here."

"I would be honoured to—"

We were interrupted by the plaintive wail of the indri.

"Excuse me, please," Hery said, answering the phone. He spoke for a moment, cupped the phone and smiled. "My mother," he whispered. "She wants to know if I'm *presentable* – in case there is a *photo opportunity*." He returned to his phone call.

"Yes, Mother... No, Mother... Yes, Mother... No, Mother..."

The photographer, a tall young black woman, cleared her throat.

"I have to go now, Mother." Hery ended his call and joined us for the photograph.

Mum, Hayley, Dad stood in the back. Crouching in front was Hery, with me on one side and Natalie on the other.

The photographer lifted her camera. "Everyone bring a smile today?" We nodded cheerfully.

"Good," said the photographer. "Then everybody say—"

"Wait!" said Natalie, pulling out a familiar green face from behind her back. "Zecko wants to say it!"

Natalie held the puppet high in the air.

"Everyb-b-body s-s-s-s-say-"

"CH-CH-CH-CH-CHEESE!"

Lightning Source UK Ltd.
Milton Keynes UK
UKHW011035021021
391551UK00002B/55